CRITICAL ACCLAIM FOR JEREMIAH HEALY AND SO LIKE SLEEP

"WELL-PACED AND ABSORBING, ENLIVENED BY A SLEW OF GRITTY CHARACTERS AND SHARPLY REALIZED LOCALES, *SO LIKE SLEEP* IS HEALY'S BEST TO DATE."

—*Kirkus Reviews*

"GRIPPING . . . LUCID . . . CUDDY HIMSELF IS A WELL-IMAGINED HERO WITH A GOOD BIT OF CHARM."

—*Boston Globe*

"ONE OF THE BEST-WRITTEN SERIES IN THE FIELD TODAY."

—*Bloomsbury Review*

"CUDDY IS AN APPEALING ADDITION TO THE GROWING NUMBER OF BOSTON DETECTIVES. . . . THE ENDING IS A SHOCKER."

—*Library Journal*

"JEREMIAH HEALY MOVES INTO THE TOP RANKS OF PRIVATE EYE WRITERS."

—*Orlando Sentinel*

D1053641

Books by Jeremiah Healy

Right to Die
So Like Sleep
The Staked Goat
Yesterday's News

Published by POCKET BOOKS

Most Pocket Books are available at special quantity discounts for bulk purchases for sales promotions, premiums or fund raising. Special books or book excerpts can also be created to fit specific needs.

For details write the office of the Vice President of Special Markets, Pocket Books, 1230 Avenue of the Americas, New York, New York 10020.

SO LIKE SLEEP

Jeremiah Healy

POCKET BOOKS

New York   London   Toronto   Sydney   Tokyo   Singapore

This book is a work of fiction. Names, characters, places, and incidents are either the product of the author's imagination or are used fictitiously. Any resemblance to actual events or locales or persons, living or dead, is entirely coincidental.

POCKET BOOKS, a division of Simon & Schuster Inc.
1230 Avenue of the Americas, New York, NY 10020

Copyright © 1987 by Jeremiah Healy

All rights reserved, including the right to reproduce
this book or portions thereof in any form whatsoever.
For information address Harper & Row, Publishers, Inc.,
10 East 53rd Street, New York, NY 10022

ISBN: 0-671-74328-7

First Pocket Books printing July 1988

10 9 8 7 6 5 4 3 2

POCKET and colophon are registered trademarks of
Simon & Schuster Inc.

Cover art by Punz Wolf;
design by Irving Freeman

Printed in the U.S.A.

For Jeremiah and Joseph

So Like Sleep

ONE

I sipped the Stroh's and stared at the roller in the aluminum pan. The door to the hall and both windows in the office were open, but the breezeless May afternoon still sealed in the paint smell. I was wearing a red T-shirt and the khaki shorts I had wine-stained the week before. The edge of the desk was hard on my rear end, the clear plastic drop cloth squeaking each time I squirmed to get comfortable. The landlord had said a two-year lease would be four hundred a month, three-eighty if I painted it myself. My former apartment-office had been burned out, and I decided the time had come to have one of each.

I turned my head and took in the view of the Boston Common, our answer to Central Park, that had hooked me on this place for the office part. At my corner of the Common is the Park Street subway station, a human kaleidoscope. In the early morning you get the rush-hour crowd, lawyers and bankers in two-piece suits, secretaries in half-salary outfits. In late morning come teachers and parent assistants leading field trips of fourth graders, lunchboxes clanking and name tags fluttering. At midday, young management trainees and salespeople picnic on the grass with sausage sandwiches, fresh fruit, or salads bought from wagoned vendors. At all hours, the Hare Krishnas chant, the past-prime folk singers strum, the bullhorn evangelists exhort. Only the winos are quiet, lying on their sides like half-opened, human jackknives. All in all, a view that could keep you sane. At least by comparison.

I swallowed another mouthful of the Stroh's and wondered for the hundredth time what "fire-brewed" means. I looked up at the half-painted walls and down again at the roller and pan. I finished the beer, flexed my rolling arm, and went back to work.

"Good to see a man with a trade." A deep, familiar voice from the doorway.

"You the guy from the lettering company?" I said without turning. "I've decided on 'John Francis Cuddy, Confidential Investigations.' "

He snorted a laugh, rapping a knuckle on the lavatory-glass section of the door. "Maybe you'd do better to leave 'Avery Stein, Tax Preparer' up here."

I laid the roller back into the pan and gestured toward the Lil' Oscar cooler on the desk. "Have a beer, Lieutenant?"

"No, thanks." Murphy came slowly into the room, careful of his clothes around the shiny walls. Shorter and heavier than I am, Murphy was the first black detective lieutenant on the force, appointed when an otherwise bigoted city councillor mistook surname for race.

I pulled a drop cloth from one of the chairs I had bid on at a liquidator's auction. "Sit."

He lightly touched the arms, seat, and back for wet spots, then settled in. "This is a pretty nice setup."

"Thank you."

He fidgeted a bit. I hadn't known him long, but I had never seen him ill at ease before.

"Can I help you with something, Lieutenant?"

He frowned, rested his elbow on the chair arm, and bothered his teeth with an index finger. "I don't like asking favors," he said.

I thought back a few months. "I figure I owe you one."

"The shotgun thing."

"Yeah."

"I guess you're right, but I still don't like asking."

I shrugged. We waited.

He made up his mind. "A woman I dated a long time ago. Her son is in deep shit, and I want you to check it out."

"As in 'get him out'?"

"Or maybe just confirm that he belongs there."

"In the deep shit."

"Yeah."

"What's the situation?"

"The name William Daniels mean anything to you?"

"Yes," I said. "But I don't place it."

"About three weeks ago. Young black shoots his white girlfriend, then confesses to their therapy group."

"The kid under hypnosis."

"That's right."

I thought back to the television reports. The arraignment, Massachusetts allowing cameras in the courtroom for some years now. Daniels, a college student, his mother holding back tears. The dead girl's father, sitting stoically, his wife back home under sedation. Ironically, the father

11

was a TV station manager who had fought for coverage of court proceedings.

"I remember some of it," I said. "Daniels had the gun on him, right?"

"The therapy witnesses say he reached into his pocket and laid it on his lap. Papers said Ballistics made it as the murder weapon."

I thought back again. "The shooting was out in Calem?"

"Uh-huh."

"In Middlesex County."

"Right."

"Not your jurisdiction."

Murphy cleared his throat. "Right again."

"But you must have official contacts out there?"

"Yeah, and if I got contacts there, why do I need to drag in a PI to tell me what I can find out myself."

"That's what I was wondering."

Murphy leaned forward, elbows on knees, hands working a little on each other. "How many black cops you think work Calem?"

"Maybe one?"

"That's right. A rookie patrolman. Two, if you count a uniformed dispatcher."

"So if you call out there, it looks like professional big-city black cop checking up on small-town white cops?"

"To see if they're 'roading a black defendant through their white suburban system." Murphy sat back, not quite relaxed.

"He must have a lawyer by now," I said.

"Private, but he used to be a Mass Defender"—meaning an attorney from the Massachusetts Defenders Committee, the old name for the Commonwealth's public defender system.

"I'd have to start with him."

"Start with the mother instead. She approves of you, she'll tell William and he'll okay it with the lawyer."

"You know the kid?"

"Met him once in a supermarket, maybe ten years ago."

I didn't ask the follow-up question, but Murphy answered it for me.

"Yeah, I think he did it. But I want Willa to think so too."

"Willa's his mother?"

"Right."

"You have her address and telephone?"

He pulled a folded paper from inside his coat and handed it to me. Willa Daniels, home and work. Robert J. Murphy, home and work.

"Thanks, Cuddy," said Murphy, rising.

"Lieutenant?"

"Yeah?"

"Why me?"

"Why you?"

"Yeah. I can't be the only private detective you know."

"Cuddy, you're the only white private detective I know who owes me a favor. I hate asking for favors. I hate owing them even more."

He slammed "Avery Stein, Tax Preparer" on the way out.

TWO

My watch was in my sports jacket on the coat tree. Rather than wipe my splattered hands, I leaned out the window. The clock on the Park Street Church tower said 2:20 P.M. It was typically five minutes slow. I already had a phone in the office, but I decided to finish the paint job and call Mrs. Daniels later.

By four-thirty, I was in the men's, scrubbing my fingers with a small brush and turpentine. A white-collar worker came in, relieved himself, and thought better of telling me I was in an executive washroom. He left without rinsing his hands.

By four forty-five, I was out of the painting clothes and back into my buttoned-down yellow shirt, tweed coat, and khaki pants. I made sure I had the piece of paper Murphy had given me and used the stairs down to the street.

I crossed Tremont and slipped sideways through the

crush of federal and state employees beating everyone else's office workers to the subway entrance. Once I was past the station, the Common sprawled green in front of me. I walked toward home.

The case that destroyed my old apartment had landed me in the hospital. After I got out, a friend suggested I call his sister. The sister, a doctor, was taking a two-year program in Chicago and needed a tenant for her condominium in Back Bay. Fortunately, the case also provided me with a chunk of money, which, when added to the insurance proceeds from the fire, allowed me to afford the rents on both the condo and the office. I could afford time too. Time to think about Nancy Meagher.

Nancy was an assistant district attorney for Suffolk County, basically meaning Boston. She was also the first woman I'd felt close to, felt anything for, since my wife, Beth, died of cancer.

At Charles Street I took the Commonwealth Avenue extension through the Public Garden. The Common is for ball playing and dog running. The Garden is for swan boating and love walking. Nancy and I hadn't walked through the Garden yet. I hoped we would. But first she would have to call me. At the hospital, she had said she needed time to think, as well. Time to think about having killed a man.

I started up Commonwealth for two blocks, shifting to Marlborough for two more, and then onto Beacon for the last block to Fairfield. If there is a better way of commuting than walking to and from work, I can't imagine it.

The condo is one of eight one-bedroom units in an old corner brownstone. It occupies the rear of the second floor on the lefthand side of the street, which means southern exposure. The living room has seven stained-glass windows across its south wall and a polished oak-front fireplace along its east wall. High-ceilinged and airy, it's the nicest place I ever lived in alone.

I took off my sports jacket and glanced at the new telephone tape machine. The Calls window displayed a fluorescent green "0," meaning no messages.

Fishing out Murphy's paper, I called Willa Daniels at both work and home. No answer at either.

I popped a steak into the broiler and took a half-full bottle of cabernet sauvignon out of the fridge to warm back down to room temperature. As dinner cooked, I drank some ice water with a twist of lime while I read most of the *New York Times,* which I had delivered each morning but usually didn't read until evening.

After I ate, I got Mrs. Daniels at home. She asked if I could come right over. She gave me an address in Roxbury and detailed directions. I said I would see her in half an hour.

I usually wear a handgun over my right buttock, but that night I undid my belt and slipped on a holstered Smith & Wesson Chief's Special so that it rode at my left front. A car carrying whites had been stoned at a traffic light in Roxbury the prior week, and if necessary, I wanted to be able to cross-draw easily.

I followed Tremont Street deep into Roxbury, making the two right and one left turns to Millrose Street. On the Danielses' block were four beautifully kept houses, three burned-out shells, and six that fell in between. The Daniels house was an in-betweener.

I spotted a parking space and maneuvered my old Fiat 124 around some barely identifiable trash and intact but empty wine bottles. The container law in Massachusetts rewards scavengers a nickel for each beer or tonic receptacle, whether glass, plastic, or aluminum, but nothing for wine jugs. A pity.

As I got out of the car, I saw three young blacks on a stoop between me and the Daniels house. All wore sleeveless athletic shirts, racing-stripe gym shorts, and sneakers. Two had socks, one didn't. They had a blaster radio turned down low on an R and B tune I didn't recognize.

As I drew even with them, the biggest of the three stood up and took a step toward me. Not threatening. Just an approach.

"Five bucks," he said.

"Five bucks?"

"To watch your car, man."

"So no harm comes to it?"

"That's right."

"Well," I said, "I'm doing a favor tonight. Ms. Daniels' son is in some trouble, and I told a friend I'd stop by and try to help."

One of the other kids on the stoop spoke. "Figured you here about Willie-boy."

"William Daniels is the name I was given."

"Ten bucks," said the original negotiator.

"Ten?" I said.

"Fifteen," said the negotiator.

I folded my arms. "You got something against young Daniels?"

"Yeah," said the stooper. "We got something against him."

"What?" I asked.

The third guy spoke for the first time. "You the Man?"

Negotiator said, "That wreck ain't no cop car."

"Could be his private wheels," said the third, defensively.

I said, "Cops are better paid than that. I'm a private investigator, just trying to help."

"What for?" said Negotiator.

"For a friend, like I said. Now, what do you have against Daniels?"

"He try to be white," said Stooper.

"Try hard," said Third.

"Suburban white pussy and all," said Stooper.

"All the good it done him," said Negotiator.

"Well," I said, "I'm not doing him much good here." I continued toward the Daniels house.

"Hey?" said Negotiator.

"Hey what?" I said over my shoulder.

"What about our bread?"

"Your bread?"

"Yeah," said Third.

"Our ten," said Stooper.

"Our fifteen," corrected Negotiator.

"Fellas," I said, climbing the Daniels steps, "it's been great talking with you." I tried the outer door. It opened. "But I'm not paying you a dime to watch my car."

"The fuck you ain't," said Negotiator.

"You're young yet," I said. "You'll get over it."

I entered the building's foyer.

The inner door cracked ajar after my second knock. Through three lock chains, a middle-aged black woman with a pretty face gave me an uncertain smile.

"Mr. Cuddy?"

"That's right."

"Please come in."

She led me into a small living room. The exterior of the house didn't do the interior justice. The wood furniture was old, solid, and polished. The upholstered furniture was bright and doilied. There was a marble mantel, with pink cherub tile around the hearth. A tray with china cups and saucers, a matching teapot, and a glass Chemex coffee pitcher was centered on a 1930s inlaid coffee table.

"Please sit down. Would you like tea or coffee?"

I don't usually drink either, but given her trouble, I said, "Tea, please. Sugar, no milk."

"Lemon?"

"No, thanks."

We remained silent while she poured. She took coffee. Her hands trembled a little, but she didn't spill any.

I tasted my tea, complimented her. She told me the name, but it was nearly unpronounceable and immediately forgotten.

I said, "Lieutenant Murphy asked me to speak with you."

She sipped her coffee, put it down. "It . . . He's good to ask you, but it . . . it's just so hard to talk about it."

"Maybe it'd be easier if you could tell me something about your son. Do you call him William?"

"Yes, William. His full name is William Everett Daniels—my father's name was Everett. My husband left us when William was just four. He was already smart enough to be hurt by that, but at least I had a good job, secretary in an insurance agency. They went broke, but I got another job right away, insurance again. I've been with them, Craig and Bulley, for thirteen years now."

I remembered the name from my time as an investigator at Empire Insurance. I looked around the room for effect. "You've done well."

"Oh, this." She fluttered her hands. "This is all from my parents, really. This was their home. When my husband left us, my father and mother took William and me in. My brother—I had a brother, Thomas, but he was killed in Vietnam."

I wondered which unit and where, but said, "Go on."

"Well, William really looked up to Thomas. He was a marine and brought William little souvenirs and things.

There wasn't a lot of antiwar stuff here in Rox', too many folks had relatives in, you know, so William really got into the military stuff, said he was gonna be a marine too. Then . . .''

"Then?"

She sighed. "Then Thomas got killed. His second tour, right near the end when everything over there just seemed so, I don't know, hopeless."

"That affected William, did it?"

"Like losing his father all over again. This time, though, William went street, started hanging out with bad kids."

"I think I met a few of them on my way in."

"You did?"

"Yeah. I had the impression they were in the insurance business too."

"Insurance?"

"Car insurance. Vandalism protection."

"Oh," she said, upset. "I'm sorry, I hope everything's all right. I should have come to your office. . . ."

I held up a palm. "The car is old, and my office stinks of wet paint. Everything will be fine. Please go on."

"Well, the kids got William into a lot of trouble, police trouble, but nothing big. Shoplifting, loitering, some fights. He never hurt anybody bad, but it got to my father; he died of a heart attack. My mother too, but because of Dad, not William, you know."

"I understand."

"Well, William's stuff was small-time, but I was still scared for him, only there's just so much a woman can do alone."

"It's a big jump from street gangs to Calem."

"Oh, yes. When William was in high school, he scored very high on the standard tests. So high his friends got mad, and he got embarrassed, so he started to intentionally miss things, questions, I mean, to level himself off a little, not stand out so much. Well, one of his teachers noticed this, and she was real good with him and got him to try going to U Mass out at Columbia Point. He went and saw a psychologist there for free a lot and straightened out. It was like a salvation.''

"What was this psychologist's name?"

"Dr. Lopez. Mariah Lopez."

"M-a-r-i-a-h?"

"I think so."

"And the teacher?"

"You mean, like to talk to her?"

"Yes."

"Her name was Sheridan. Emily Sheridan. But she was retired, oh, two years back and moved to Arizona somewhere."

"Did William like U Mass?"

"Yes. He went there for two years and did real well. All his teachers just raved about him. In fact, that was kind of the problem."

"I don't get you."

"Well," she said, reaching down for the coffee cup, but then hesitating, "the teachers thought that he could do better than U Mass, and a couple of them, along with Dr. Lopez, they pushed and pulled and got him into Goreham College for his junior year."

"Fine school."

"Yes, and so expensive. But there was plenty of scholarship money, it seems."

"Did he live there?"

"I'm sorry?"

"Did he stay at Goreham? In a dormitory?"

"Oh, yes. At least, at first. Then something happened

there, he never would tell me what, and like he moved home halfway through."

"Halfway through?"

"Through his first semester there."

"How was he doing gradewise?"

She unnecessarily stirred her coffee. "Not so good. Maybe too much change. Maybe too much . . ."

"Too much . . . ?"

She looked up. "He took up with the white girl. Or maybe better to say she took up with him. I never did know which."

"The girl he's accused of killing?"

"Yes, but he didn't. He didn't kill her or anybody else." She said it evenly, like a much-quoted religious tenet she knew by heart and believed was true beyond reasonable doubt.

"The girl was shot. Your son produced the gun that killed her."

She focused on the cup and spoon again.

"Was it William's gun, Mrs. Daniels?"

"He needed it. He said 'cause of the other kids on the block here." She mimicked them: " 'White school, white girl, white Willll-yum.' " She moved her mouth as if she'd bit a sour grape.

"He carried a gun because of the other kids' taunting him?"

She fixed me with a "c'mon" stare. "You been outside here, you seen 'em."

She was probably right. They looked more like "sticks and stones will break my bones" than "words will never hurt me."

"Had William had a fight with the girl?"

She became more agitated, waving her hands in an abbreviated version of an umpire's "safe" sign. "I don't know. I just don't. He never would talk with me about her. Or about college. Goreham, I mean. Or even the new doctor he was seeing."

"What doctor was that?"

"The one who did the hypnotizing. The one where . . . where . . ." She reached for a napkin and mumbled she was sorry, exactly as I was saying it was all right.

She sniffled for a moment or two. I waited.

"Can I tell you anything else?" she asked.

"Not now. I have to read some reports first, talk with William's lawyer. I'll need you to call the lawyer, tell him I'm working for your son."

She nodded vigorously, reached for a handbag sitting on a nearby chair. "I have money. I took more out of the bank when Rob . . . Lieutenant Murphy told me you'd be coming. He said—"

"Mrs. Daniels. No money, please."

She looked up with the "c'mon" expression again. " 'Cause I didn't used to earn enough when William was younger, he qualified for the Mass Defenders. That's how he got to know Mr. Rothenberg, the lawyer he's got now for this. But I gave Mr. Rothenberg a retainer, and I want to pay you too. I never did like taking charity, and I won't take any more of it."

"Not charity. A favor. For"—I stretched it a bit—"a friend, Lieutenant Murphy. It's his favor, but you and William will be my clients. I'll talk to the lieutenant only if I need information or help."

She chewed on it for a minute. "Can you help William?" she said quietly.

"I hope so." I meant it, and I also hoped she could tell.

She gave me Rothenberg's address and phone number. I wrote down an authorizing message to leave in case he was out when she called him. I also gave her one of my new cards, writing my home number on the back.

She let me out through the chains. I had forgotten about my car. So, apparently, had the three freelancers. It was where I had left it and in one piece. I got in and drove home.

I walked in. Nothing on the tape machine. I remembered I hadn't checked the mailbox, so I went back downstairs to the foyer. Nothing again. Not many of my friends could write, and I was too recently moved in to be receiving the "You Already May Have Won" crap.

I came back upstairs, stripped, and showered. I finished the *Times* and decided to turn in. I looked at the telephone a couple of times, thinking of Nancy, then dropped off.

THREE

◆

I woke up at 7:00 A.M., with the alarm. I pulled on running shoes, shorts, and a T-shirt from an army surplus store on Boylston Street. The shirt had a small USA on the left breast. It had been on the rack next to one with a skull wearing a green beret and the legend KILL THEM ALL— LET GOD SORT THEM OUT. I bought the USA.

I limbered up for ten minutes, then jogged across the Fairfield Street bridge to the Charles River. Turning left, I ran leisurely upriver toward the Boston University bridge. I passed a cormorant floating low in the water, its black-beaked head and long neck above the surface like an organic periscope. At the bridge, I reversed direction, picking up the pace maybe thirty seconds the mile. A sixty-year-old woman blew by me as if I were standing still. Her T-shirt read GRANDMOTHERS HAVE DONE IT LONGER.

I reached Community Boating, in the shadow of the

Charles Street bridge. When I got back from the service, I had learned to sail there, a six-month, good-any-time membership costing about fifty dollars. They supplied and maintained the boats, and more-experienced members taught you rigging. It was a good deal. I fell away from it after Beth got sick; the only sailboats I noticed now were the ones plying the harbor below her gravesite.

I reversed direction again and maximized my stride, taking two short breaths and one long one for every eight steps. I stopped at the Dartmouth Street bridge, making it a four-mile run. On Newbury Street, I bought some fresh muffins and orange juice for breakfast.

Back at the condo, I warmed down, showered, and ate. The kitchen clock said eight-thirty. I called the number for William's attorney and drew a brusque female voice that said the offices didn't open till nine. She did confirm that Rothenberg was due in that morning before court in Cambridge. After dressing reasonably well, I walked the eight blocks down Boylston to Rothenberg's office, which was only two doors up from the old Mass Defenders building.

The door on Rothenberg's floor said simply LAW OF-FICES, with a dozen full names on separate, mismatched wooden plaques underneath. Likely that meant that he shared space but not fees with the eleven other attorneys. I entered a waiting room containing a grab bag of clients. The public defenders, now the Office for Public Counsel Services, typically got the good poor and the bad poor. Anyone on a higher economic rung had to scratch for private counsel. Therefore, lawyers like Rothenberg usually got the good not-so-poor and the bad not-so-poor.

I gave the receptionist my name, profession, and mission. Ten minutes later, she answered her phone, called out my name, and pointed me down a hallway, all as she tried to persuade an animated woman speaking machine-gun Spanish to slow down.

I was halfway down the hall when a balding head bobbed out of a doorway. He said, "John Cuddy?"

"That's right." He beckoned me in.

His office was cluttered and shabby but apparently all his own. We shook hands.

"Steve Rothenberg." He gestured to a chair with his free hand. He slumped into a cracked leather desk chair and put his feet up on the pullout from the old metal desk.

"What can I do for you?" he said. His beard, flecked with gray, bobbed up and down, riding the Adam's apple beneath. He wore a white buttoned-down shirt and a rep tie, but the collar was undone, the tie loosened, and the sleeves rolled up.

"I'm working for Willa Daniels. I understand you represent her son, William."

"And?"

"And I'd like to talk with you about his case."

Rothenberg frowned, tapping a pencil against a file lying on his desk blotter. "Can I see your identification?"

I showed him. He studied it, copied some information onto a pad, and gave it back to me.

"You have any references I can check?"

"Sure," I said, "but why?"

He picked up a pink phone message slip. "This was waiting for me when I got in. From Mrs. Daniels. She isn't stupid, but this sounds like somebody else wrote it for her."

"I did. Last night, so I could speak with you today." I shifted in my chair. "What's wrong?"

"When I spoke with Mrs. Daniels, I didn't have the

27

impression that she had the kind of money to have two professionals working on William's case.''

Rothenberg either was worried about getting more money or was suspicious that I might be leeching off a vulnerable relative. I gave him the benefit of the doubt. "If it helps any, I'm doing this as a favor for a friend.''

"That's kind of what I'm doing too.''

"I don't get you.''

"I represented William when he was a juvenile and I was with the Mass Defenders. You know how cases got assigned to us back then?''

"Not really.''

"Well, the short version is that we got assigned pretty regularly by some judges, not so much by others. A question of . . . attitudes.''

"By attitudes, you mean a judge's cronies who got cut out of some court-appointed fees?''

"Draw your own interpretations. Point is, almost everybody, every criminal defendant, can come up with money for private counsel somehow.''

"So?''

"So in William's case back then, the judge at arraignment didn't like us, and William was sort of borderline for indigency because of his mother's job and all. But I thought I saw something in him, something worth pushing for. So we, read I, made the pitch in open court, and the judge grudgingly assigned us.''

"And?''

"And I kept the little shit he'd stepped in from becoming big shit, and then he went off to college, and then . . .'' Rothenberg stopped, exhaling noisily.

"And then your reclamation project goes and ruins your effort by killing a girl.''

Rothenberg gritted his teeth, then relaxed. "One way of putting it."

"Then why are you helping him now?"

"Partly money, but mostly, well, when his mother contacted me, the case seemed more interesting than it does now. Legally speaking, I mean."

"How so?"

He paused, fingered the file in front of him. "My client is William, not his mother."

"Meaning?"

"Since your client is the mother, not the son, I'm not so sure I can talk with you about his case."

"What have we been talking about—Jimmy Hoffa?"

"No, I mean the merits of the case. The factual and legal arguments, my work product, conference with him, and so on."

I thought back to my year of law school. "Can't I be your necessary agent, even if one of us is working for free?"

He smiled. "That's pretty good. But the mother hired you, even without money, and that means I didn't, and therefore I don't think a court would buy you as an agent for William's lawyer."

He made no effort to end the interview, so I assumed he wanted me to try a different tack.

"Would it be a good bet that the reason William's case is uninteresting is because it's ironclad against him?"

Rothenberg, wrinkling his brow, allowed, "It'd be a good bet."

"Then there probably wouldn't be any cosmic harm if you were to go the men's room and I, without your knowledge or help, sort of skimmed Daniels' file."

Rothenberg brightened. "Hypothetically speaking, no,

no harm at all." He stood up. "Would you excuse me? I have to take a leak."

"Sure."

He closed the door behind him.

I suppose somebody could fault Rothenberg for not observing the spirit behind some of his attorney ethics. However, all he really did was save me a second trip to his office, since William could have authorized me to see his file once I saw him.

The folder Rothenberg had been playing with was marked DANIELS, WILLIAM E. I opened it.

FOUR

An intake sheet was stapled to the left inside of the folder, but the only significant fact I didn't already have was William's date of birth. He'd just turned twenty.

The bill of indictment listed two crimes. Murder in the first degree and unlawful possession of a firearm. The possession charge bespoke a thorough, if overzealous, prosecution. Even if Rothenberg somehow beat the killing, William was gone under the state's tough gun law for an automatic, no-parole one-year on the unlicensed-weapon charge. But first things first.

The victim's name was Jennifer Creasey, age eighteen years. The police report read like a synopsis of a Charlie Chan movie.

Uniformed officers Clay and Bjorkman were summoned to the office of Dr. Clifford Marek, One Professional Park, Calem. There they met Dr. Marek, who showed them in the basement a young white female, deceased, with apparent gunshot wounds to the chest, identified as Jennifer Creasey. Dr. Marek gave them a .38-caliber Smith & Wesson Detective's Special revolver, serial number 7D43387. The rounds in all six chambers had been expended.

The officers asked the source of the weapon and were taken by Dr. Marek back upstairs to William E. Daniels. Officer Clay remained with Daniels and read him his rights while Bjorkman summoned the Detective Bureau. Detectives O'Boy and Rizzi interviewed the doctor and other patients on the premises.

According to the interviews, Daniels and the decedent were members of a therapy group Marek conducted each Thursday night. Hypnosis figured prominently in the treatment, with a different group member being hypnotized by Marek each week, then being questioned by the doctor and each other member.

I shook my head. Lord, let me never be psychoanalyzed.

That night was Daniels's turn to be hypnotized and questioned. He arrived late, appeared restless, irritable. Having already waited for ten minutes, Marek began without Jennifer Creasey. After putting Daniels under, Marek began by asking, as he always did, about the subject's movements during the previous hour.

Daniels responded by saying he had shot Jennifer in the basement boiler room. When the doctor and others expressed surprise, Daniels reached into his coat pocket and laid the aforementioned weapon on his lap. One of the other patients, a Homer Linden, got up and snatched the gun away. Marek and another group member, Lainie Bishop, went down to the boiler room while Linden and the last group member, a Donald Ramelli, watched over Daniels. Marek and Ms. Bishop discovered the body and came back upstairs, by which time Ramelli had already called the police.

Short supplementary statements of each group member affirmed the consensus story. All were certain that Daniels and the decedent were having a sexual relationship.

A report from Ballistics established the revolver as the murder weapon. A second, from the medical examiner, confirmed two bullet wounds to the chest as the cause of death, with no indication of pre- or postmortem sexual activity or assault.

There were some lab results on William himself. One from the state police at 1010 Commonwealth Avenue stated that a paraffin test on William's hands showed he'd fired a weapon recently. Another said his blood tested positive for no drug except flurazepam, whatever the hell that was. The last entry in the file was from a court-ordered shrink, certifying Daniels as sane at the time of the shooting and competent to stand trial now. I took down all relevant names and addresses, then closed the folder.

Rothenberg came in just as I was putting my list into a coat pocket. He was carrying several pieces of typed paper.

"Sorry to be so long," he said brightly.

"I kept myself amused."

"Well?"

"Can we talk? In the clear, I mean?"

Rothenberg frowned, then gave me a "why not" shrug.

"What's Daniels's defense?" I said.

"That's just the trouble. When William's mother called me, I had already seen the television story on the killing."

"Go on."

"Well, we had a murder involving hypnosis. I jumped at it because of—are you up on the Commonwealth's view of hypnosis?"

"No."

"Okay." He put the papers down. "Some states' courts say a hypnotized witness can testify in court, some say he or she can't because the very act of being hypnotized can block out certain memories and create certain others. You with me?"

"So far."

"Well, our Supreme Judicial Court ruled in the *Kater* case that it would accept as competent a witness who had revealed certain facts *before* hypnosis but not facts revealed only *under* or *after* hypnosis. Okay?"

"Okay, but—"

"Let me finish. I figured we had a great test case under a footnote in *Kater*. You see, can a criminal defendant be kept off the stand, be incompetent as a witness, to tell his side of an event which would be revealed only *after* he'd been hypnotized?"

"That's what made the case seem interesting at first?"

"Right."

"So what's spoiled it?"

"This," he said, sliding the typed pages over to me.

They were a transcription of notes taken by Rothenberg at an interview he had with Daniels a week earlier at the Middlesex County detention facility in the courthouse building in Cambridge. Rothenberg talked as I read. "There are so many of us sharing a secretary here, it takes a week to get anything that isn't a life or death emergency."

I finished the transcription. If it was accurate, Daniels himself corroborated virtually every detail in the police version.

I looked up. Rothenberg said, "See?"

"I think so. Even if the trial judge would let Daniels

testify after hypnosis, Daniels would just crucify himself."

"Exactly," said Rothenberg, lacing his fingers behind his head and leaning back in his chair. He smiled at his apt pupil. "Putting Daniels on the stand would be suicide."

"And there goes the test-case part of it."

"Uh-huh."

I pushed the interview report back to him. "So now what?"

Rothenberg stopped smiling, looked resigned. "We plead him to a reduced charge. If we can."

" 'If we can'?"

"Put yourself in the DA's place. Better, in the assistant's place. The guy who'll try the case. This is worth at least eight, nine days of jury trial. Great media exposure for the trial counsel, including two minutes easy on the six o'clock news each night. Say we go with insanity, or diminished capacity. That means we're putting the kid's mental condition in issue, and that waives the patient-psychotherapist privilege. That means the jurors definitely get to hear Marek—that's his shrink—telling about the séance with the gun. Oh, the judge has to instruct the jury to consider the testimony only on the issue of Daniels' mental condition, and not on his doing the shooting, but no jury alive can keep those things separate. Also, the trial then becomes a forum for everybody to rail about the insanity defense, John Hinckley, the safety of our streets, et cetera, et cetera. I think the court-ordered report'll stand up. I've talked to this Marek, and briefly to his former shrink, some U Mass staffer."

"Dr. Lopez?"

"Yes, that's her." He went from resigned to gloomy. "No, we all think he was and is legally sane, so to speak."

"Does that mean that if you don't plead insanity, you can keep out his confession at the 'séance'?"

"Maybe, maybe not. His story itself was after hypnosis, so that ought to stay out. But does the patient-psychotherapist privilege include the therapy group members, does it include his physical agitation, his taking the murder weapon out of his pocket? No, with the circumstantial stuff this strong, not to mention the black boy–white girl angle, nineteen juries out of twenty will convict. In an hour. They'll stay out three to make it look good, like they really wrestled with the case. But they'll convict."

"Any chance of bail?"

"No. Oh, the arraignment judge set bail at three hundred thousand surety, thirty thousand cash alternative. But Mrs. Daniels can't swing either. I'd bet my retainer, which was half what I should have taken, nearly tapped her out as it is." He looked down at his watch. "I've got to run. Anything else?"

"Yeah. Can you get me in to see Daniels at Middlesex?"

"I guess," he said—wondering, no doubt, how big a favor I must be repaying.

FIVE

Rothenberg and I rattled to Lechmere on the Green Line subway and walked the three blocks to the tall, modern courthouse facility. Rothenberg flashed his Board of Bar Overseers card at the Middlesex County Police security team on the first floor. I had to go through the metal detector.

We rode the first elevator to the seventeenth floor. Rothenberg vouched for me with the Sheriff's Department correctional officer inside the thick-windowed control center, then left for his court appearance downstairs. I completed a "Request to Visit Inmate" form and fed it with my photo ID to the officer through a Diebold tray like a drive-up bank's. He returned a blue and white visitor's pass, which I clipped onto my lapel.

The officer waved me to the entrance trap. A red heavy-metal door slid open, unsealing one end of the trap. I entered and cleared another metal detector. Then, and only after the first door chunked closed, the officer opened the second door, admitting me to the visitors' area. I sat in a glassed-in room on an old but surprisingly comfortable green Leatherette chair.

Ten minutes later, a husky guard escorted to me a slim black man I recognized from the television tapes to be William Daniels. Dressed in a medium-green inmate's shirt and faded green trousers, Daniels had the graceful gait and fine-featured face of a young Arthur Ashe. He eyed me warily as I stood to shake his hand, the guard closing the door as he left but moving back to a position from which he could watch over us.

"My name is John Cuddy. I'm a private investigator. I told your mother I would look into your case."

Daniels ignored my outstretched hand. Taking the seat across from me, he squinted and sneered. "You choose your words real careful, don't you?"

"I try to," I said, dropping my hand and sitting back down.

"What you didn't say was that my mama's pig friend asked you to check me out so you could tell her I'm guilty."

"You're smart enough to know that the more help you get, the better off you are."

He laughed. "Yeah, right. Well, let me save you a lot of your freely given time. I did it. I remember doing it. And I'm glad I did it." He didn't look glad.

"Look, I—"

"So just leave it, huh? Just leave it and me be!"

His voice rose enough at the end for the guard to come forward two steps. I shook my head, and the guard withdrew cautiously.

Daniels's expression was sullen, pouty. "Would it hurt anything," I said, "for you to tell me what happened?"

"You know, I don't have to talk with you at all. I can just stand up and walk, anytime."

"I know. You can walk over to the officer there, who'll take you back to protective custody or general population or wherever it is they stack you. Then you'll wait for Rothenberg to try to grovel a reduction in charge. Maybe he can even parlay it into a sentence that'll get you a shot at parole, like around the turn of the century."

"The fuck do you know about it?"

"Not much. That's why I'm here."

He turned his face down a notch. "Look, you're wastin' your time. They got me. Every which way. My girl, my gun, fuckin' roomful of witnesses. Shit, they put this one on TV, the show'd be canceled. No drama."

"I don't think you've gotten the idea," I said gently. "See, you're supposed to tell me your side of it, then I dig around and—"

"Aw, man, what kinda shit you slingin'? My side *is* their side. I done it, man. They got me and they know it. And no smilin' Irish face gonna change that."

"William . . ." I started, but he had already stood and turned away from me, motioning to the guard that he was finished.

As I rode the subway back into Boston, I tried to make up my mind about what I should do. Easiest was to call Murphy, tell him I had confirmed William's guilt, then break the news of my exit to Mrs. Daniels. The more I thought about it, the less easy that path appeared. All I had done was read a few reports, talk with a disappointed defense attorney, and bungle a client interview. Not exactly a thorough, professional effort.

On the other hand, I could spend three or four days chasing after the names in the report. Then I could check each one off as he or she substantiated what everybody but Mrs. Daniels believed. That her son shot Jennifer Creasey.

While our train was stopped inexplicably in a tunnel, I decided to call Murphy and tell him the kid wouldn't talk to me. Then Murphy could try to get Mrs. Daniels to persuade William again. If that failed, I'd be off the hook.

I felt better and looked at my watch. Eleven-twenty. Plenty of time to pick up the car and visit before calling Murphy.

"I don't know if I like the green paper as well."

The roses were yellow, small but open flowers, sharp but widely spaced thorns. I bent over and laid them lengthwise to her.

"Mrs. Feeney says the company that manufactured the white tissue went bust, and the new outfit would charge her fifty percent more for the white."

I smoothed the paper down. It crinkled. The old paper, the white, sort of whispered.

Don't worry about it, said Beth. *What do you think you're doing, working a toilet paper commercial?*

I laughed. I looked past her stone to the Daugherty plot. His monument was granite, not marble, and some of the blood from last March was still dried dark on it. I stopped smiling and repressed a shudder.

Have you heard from Nancy?

"No. I thought about calling her, but . . ."

You're probably right not to push it.

"I know."

She needs time, John.

"I know that too."

There was nothing more to say on that subject. The sky

40

was overcast, the air still. No sailboats in our part of the harbor. Two Boston Whalers raced on a near-collision course, both heading toward an anchored third, already bucking, its fishing rods bending.

"New case, Beth. Son of a friend of the police lieutenant who covered for me last time. They say the son shot his girlfriend."

Who says?

"That's the problem. Everybody. The son included."

What do you say?

"I don't know. He isn't helping me very much."

How old is he?

"Only twenty, but a smart kid. Goreham College."

Is that where he met the girlfriend?

"I think so."

Why would a rich Goreham boy want to kill a rich girl?

"Well, to start with, he's not rich. He's a black scholarship student. Her family, a white family, seems pretty well off, though."

Did he love her?

"He didn't say." I thought for a minute. "No question that he caught a lot of flak from the neighborhood kids—black kids—about her, and he seems pretty intense, so yeah, I'd say he must have loved her to put up with it."

You said he wasn't helping you much.

"That's right."

If you had lost me when you were twenty, and everybody said you were at fault, would you be much help to you?

I swallowed. "I lost you when I was a lot older than twenty, and I knew the cancer wasn't my fault, and I still wasn't much help to anybody."

She waited a moment. *See?*

I saw. "Her name was Jennifer Creasey," I said.

I'll watch for her.

41

SIX

When you need information, talk to someone who gathers it for a living. The *Boston Herald*'s newsroom was noisy, in a muted sort of way. The screaming of editors and clattering of standard typewriters had yielded to the squawking of intercoms and the burping of computer terminals. I preferred the old atmosphere myself, and I know Mo Katzen did too.

He was in his office, as always, in the ill-fitting vest and trousers of a three-piece suit, as always.

"Mo, how can you be a reporter, yet never be out on a story?"

"Hah, tell me about it," he said, teeth clamped on a comatose cigar. He gestured toward the aged Remington that he still insisted on using. "You know what I'm writing about?"

"No, Mo. I—"

"A desk." The top of his own desk looked like the step-off point of a ticker-tape parade. He took the cigar from his mouth. "A fifty-year-old desk that Mayor Curley supposedly had—there's no supposed about it; I saw him perched on it often enough with these." He pointed the index and middle fingers of his free hand at his eyes. "But no, the lawyers say we got to say 'supposedly.' Anyway, I'm writing about this desk that Curley supposedly had, that through the regimes Mayor White supposedly received, and that Mayor Flynn now wants to sit behind—no supposing there. Flynn really wants the desk. And guess what?"

"Nobody can find it?"

"On the button, John," he said, inhaling as he futilely tried to get a throwaway lighter to fire his stogie. "Nobody can find a carved wood desk that's got maybe thirty pounds on the *Andrea Doria.*"

"Mo, I—"

"Goddamn thing," said Mo, pitching the lighter toward his wastebasket but missing. "You're supposed to write with their pens, and shave with their razors, and you can't get their goddamned lighters to spark enough to fry a moth."

"Mo—"

"Getting back to the desk, though. There's got to be five hundred—no, call it five thousand desks in City Hall. Every brother-in-law who's on the payroll eventually gets a promotion into some created slot to free up *his* spot for the next brother-in-law. And if you promote the guy, you've gotta give him a desk, right?"

"Right."

"Of course, right. I mean, the raise in pay, the change in title, those aren't enough. The expansion of duties and

43

responsibilities sure can't carry it. What's two times zero? Zero, am I right?''

"Math always was your strong—''

"But with these five thousand desks and five thousand brothers-in-law, the city's crack investigators can't find Hizzoner's desk. You know they're turning City Hall upside down? Looking at everybody's desk. Looking *inside* the things, for God's sake. Like Curley's desk was maybe a stolen racehorse, and somebody rubbed on shoe polish to cover the star on its forehead. I tell you, John, it makes me sick."

"Sick is right, Mo. I—''

"And you'd think, wouldn't you, you'd think that the new administration would have the sense to do all this hush-hush? I mean, between Proposition Two and a Half wrecking the budget, and busing wrecking the schools, and potholes wrecking anything with wheels, you'd think that the administration wouldn't want to advertise that it's got more guys on this desk thing than the city did on the Boston Strangler. But no, they've got to let the media in on it, which means TV covered it last night, which means I got to have this ready by . . . Oh, I'm telling you, John, every time I think about it, I get sick."

"Mo, before I call for an ambulance—''

"Ambulance?''

"Before I—''

"Who said anything about an ambulance?''

"Nobody did, Mo. It—''

"You better watch yourself, John." He pointed the cigar at me. "I think your mind's beginning to wander."

I asked Mo if I could see the paper's morgue information on the Creasey case. The *Herald*'s got the best criminal coverage in the city, but after an hour's reading, the only new information I found was that the Federal Communications Commission was leaning against renewing the license of the television station run by the dead girl's father. Some days you get the peanuts, some days you get the shells.

SEVEN

I stopped at a push-button pay phone and dialed my own home number. I waited for the ringing to stop and the outgoing tape to start. I punched in my code number and heard two messages whir backward in Donald Duck talk. The first message was from Mrs. Daniels, asking me to call her at home that evening. The second was from Murphy, telling me to call him at home that evening.

I pressed a few more buttons to reset the tape machine, then checked in with my answering service. Same two messages.

I hung up and tried Dr. Clifford Marek. I told his receptionist that I had read about his work with hypnosis and hoped he could help me with "my problem." She said ordinarily two weeks' notice would be necessary but reluctantly admitted a fortuitous cancellation for 3:30 P.M.

I accepted with what I hoped were sufficient sounds of gratitude.

I had a burger and two beers at a pub around the corner from the *Herald*. Then I drove out to Calem.

I didn't know the town well, but Marek's address was right at the edge of the municipal center and recessed from the road. The building was four stories high, yellow brick. The lobby was simple and empty. The directory listed a group dental practice on the first floor, two podiatrists on the second, three pediatricians on the third, and just Marek on the fourth. Nice suburban professional atmosphere. There was a STAIRS door to the left of the directory. I walked over and tried the knob. The door opened, and I slipped through it onto a concrete staircase with blue metal railing. It appeared to lead up to the offices and down to the basement.

I went down fifteen steps to a second door, also unlocked, but marked BASEMENT—NO ADMISSION. Behind the second door was a hallway with three doors on the left side, spaced equidistantly. An elevator and two other doors occupied the right side. Four of the five doors said STORAGE and were secured. The fifth door said HVAC, short for "Heating, Ventilating, and Air Conditioning." The "boiler room." It was ajar and music drifted through the opening. I walked quietly to it.

A man in a brown maintenance worker's jumpsuit was fiddling at the base of some machinery against one wall. A small and battered transistor radio managed to spew an instrumental piece that was supposed to be "easy listening." The man clanged a tool against a pipe and cursed.

"This where the girl died?" I said.

The guy jumped, startled. He was maybe fifty, five-six, and one seventy or so. I started to apologize, but he cut me off.

"What're you doin' here? It says 'No Admittance,' y'know."

"My mother's upstairs. At the dentist's. The drilling noise drives me nuts. I had to get away from it."

"Huh," said the guy, giving a half laugh, wiping his perspiring face with the back of his hand. "Try workin' here. Cleaning the floor, you can't get away from it through three closed doors. Fuckin' bastard built this building, he didn't care about soundproofing. Down here, it's solid, quiet. Up there, a madhouse. You'd think the dentists'd complain."

"They probably don't notice it."

"Huh." The half laugh again. "You're probably right. Never thought about that. They wouldn't, would they?"

"The girl from the TV, the shrink case—this where she was killed?"

"Christ," said the guy, crossing himself, "don't remind me, huh. It gives me the creeps just bein' in here. That's why the radio. Fuckin' music's shit, but at least it's noise."

"Were you here when it happened?"

"Naw. Happened at night. I knock off at four. I got another building to cover for the management company. They'd have me doing ten buildings if they could, save a dime." He gestured toward a corner where the floor was both more stained and more freshly scrubbed. There were patch marks on the cement wall above it, as if someone had spackled over nail holes left by the previous tenant. "Over there's where she got it. Stupid cunt. Playin' around with a nigger. She was good family, shoulda known better."

I let his comment pass and said, "You do the floor?"

"Yeah, once the cops okayed it. The walls too, 'count of the bullets. The floor, huh, company said it wanted it to look the same. I ask you, you ever try to clean blood offa concrete?''

"No."

"Well, it don't. It don't ever clean. It's like God never meant for it to go away." He looked back over toward it, almost reverently. "Never'll look right."

"You knew her?"

"Who?"

"The girl. Did you know her?"

"No."

"You said she was from a good family. I thought maybe . . ."

"Naw, naw. That was from the news. The tube. Her father owns the TV station or something."

"You ever see her before?"

"Just when she come to see Marek. She was the kind always took the elevator, never the stairs. Great looker, but never said hello or nothin'. You know the type."

"You know Marek at all?"

"Huh, hear some pretty funny noises comin' from his . . ." He stopped. "You seem mighty interested in all this."

I glanced at my watch. Nearly three-thirty.

"About time to check on Mom anyway. Good luck on the machinery."

He shook the wrench at the unit. "Fuckin' management company. Won't pay for a service contract. Want me to fix the thing. Save a dime, you know?"

I nodded, wondering as I left him why a member of a Thursday evening group like the Creasey girl would ever come to see Marek early enough for the superintendent to see her before "knocking off at four."

I climbed the stairs to the fourth floor. Marek's doorway swung into a waiting area with the usual arrangement,

49

except the chairs were leather, not plastic, and the carpets Oriental. The brown-haired, middle-aged receptionist took my name, appraised me in some paraprofessional way, and told me to please have a seat. Picking up the telephone, she buzzed, then spoke briefly into it.

The chair was comfortable. The magazines, fanned symmetrically on a knee-high table, included *Town & Country, Architectural Digest,* and, saints preserve us, *Ducks Unlimited.* I had counted four back issues of the last when the inside door opened and a handsome, barrel-chested man of about forty-five came out, smiling. He had bushy hair the color of a nicotine stain, whitening at the mustache, eyebrows, and sideburns. He extended a hand, and we shook warmly.

"Mr. Cuddy. I'm Clifford Marek. Do come in." To the brunette he said, "Mrs. Porter, no calls, please."

He ushered me into an expansive room with wood-framed diplomas and original prints on the wall and a deep-blue Persian rug on the floor. There was an impressive array of electronic equipment on bookshelves behind his desk. The desk itself was dark mahogany and very familiar. I placed it as a twin of the one that Regional Head of Claims had at Empire. Most of his subordinates assumed he owned it. His secretary had told me he only rented it. Maybe Marek had similar pretensions.

"Please," he said, indicating a black leather armchair that was a little brother to his executive-model desk chair.

We sat. He unscrewed a fountain pen and let it hover over a clean legal pad on his desk. "Just a few preliminaries. Other psychiatrists usually relegate these to their staff, but I've always believed a professional should know his patients from the ground up, so to speak."

"Six-two and a bit."

He hesitated. "Six-two . . . ?"

"And a bit. That's me, from the ground up. So to speak."

He laughed politely but without mirth. "Good to see you've a sense of humor, sir."

"I hope it's reciprocated."

"I beg your . . ."

"Frankly, Doctor, I'm here on somewhat false pretenses. I'm not a prospective patient, though I do have a problem. With the Creasey matter."

Marek made a ceremony of recapping his pen. "I'm afraid I've accorded about as much time as I can spare for press interviews, so if you'll—"

"I'm not a reporter, Doctor. I'm a private investigator." I showed him my identification. "I'm trying to help a former patient of yours, William Daniels."

Marek allowed his features to fall. He sighed deeply, a great father figure for a soap opera.

"A tragic young man, but I've already done all I can for him."

"Perhaps—"

"You are acquainted with a Mr. Rothenberg, I presume?"

"Yes."

"I've already spoken to him. By telephone, granted, but I really, *really,* can't help you."

"Doctor, what I need to know—"

"Mr. Cuddy, please, a moment." Marek lowered his voice, sharing a secret with an obviously trustworthy stranger. "Have you ever heard of the *Tarasoff* case?"

My day for continuing legal education. "No."

He warmed to it. "Simplified, it was a California case in which a psychotherapist was sued for failing to warn a girl or her parents that a male patient was threatening to

51

kill her. The patient killed the girl, and the court allowed the parents to bring the suit.''

"And you're afraid that the Creasey girl's parents might sue you?"

"Just so. Of course, there is no precedent for such a suit in Massachusetts, and I knew, learned, of nothing from William that would have, that could have, led me to believe he would do anything to hurt Jennifer, but, well, one can't be too careful.''

"You said that you gave press interviews?"

"Yes.''

"Can't you tell me what you told them?"

"Certainly," said Marek, opening his hands like a priest in benediction. "But that was a description of what happened in the group session. William's confession, that is.'' Marek arranged his mouth to appear rueful. "I'm sure there are some who would criticize me for doing so, but I could not hope to muzzle the rest of the therapy group, and I wanted William to have the benefit of at least an accurate account of what happened.''

"That was good of you," I said with a straight face.

Marek gave a joyless laugh. "The ironic aspect of this whole matter is that through the media coverage, the marvelous advantages of hypnosis in therapy are being widely publicized. As Mrs. Porter no doubt told you, only a late cancellation even allowed . . . But I digress. There is really nothing I can tell you that will help. William, that is.''

So to speak. I tried a different approach. "May I see the room where the group session was held?"

"The room?" He thought about it. "I can see no help for you there.''

"Any harm in indulging me?"

"Well. . ." Marek looked to the grandfather clock face up to the left.

"For the sake of two former patients?"

The Shakespearean sigh again. "If you wish."

He rose. I followed through a doorway that led into a squarish room, furnished mostly with a circle of chairs and one in the middle. The chair in the middle faced the doorway we used. There was a low table near one of the chairs. A second interior door opened onto a bathroom, and a closed third door, if I had my directions right, would lead back into the reception foyer.

"As I said, there isn't much to see."

"Any changes since that night?"

"Changes? No."

"William sat in the center chair?"

"That's right. The member being hypnotized that night would sit there, the other members and I in the circle."

"Where did you sit?"

"Where I always do," said Marek, pointing to the chair nearest the low table.

"What's the table's purpose?"

"Purpose?"

"Yeah, what does it do that makes you always sit next to it?"

"Well, That's where . . . the table holds the syringe with the flurazepam. As well as, of course, other items should a patient become . . . well, too excited."

"One of the lab reports said William tested positive for flurazepam. What exactly is it?"

"You would call it a relaxant. It simply enhances the subject's chances of a successful hypnosis."

I expect I frowned, because Marek said, "Is something wrong?"

"You both drug and hypnotize the patient?"

"That's correct."

"Isn't that kind of like wearing both a belt and suspenders?"

"No, not at all. The drug and the hypnosis are complementary aides to successful therapy."

"When do you administer the drug?"

"Just a few minutes before the session begins. It works quickly and is quite harmless."

"The other patients are here when you inject the night's subject?"

"Yes. Originally, I did that so new members would be able to see how painless and easy the entire process was. Now I suppose I just do it from . . . oh, habit."

"Then after you inject the patient, everybody gets to ask questions?"

"Well," said Marek, a bit defensively, "it's considerably more monitored than that. I channel and redirect the session at various points in various ways."

"Did you have many new members?"

"I beg your pardon?"

"New members. Turnover in the therapy group."

"Oh, no, the group was quite stable." A wink. "No pun intended." The sigh again. "Of course, now, with two members gone, and given the circumstances, I've been seeing the remaining members privately."

"Do you plan to start the group up again?"

"Perhaps. After a time."

I walked to the center chair, turned, and sat in it. Marek looked down at me. I looked up and past him to the doorway. There was a video camera mounted above it. The lens seemed pointed at me.

"Is the camera focused on this chair?"

Marek half turned, came back smiling. "Yes, yes it is. I often tape the sessions. It permits more thorough analysis of difficulties and more vivid demonstrations of progress.''

"Did you videotape William's group often?"

"Yes. You see, that group was truly an experiment. Indeed, an experiment within an experiment, if you will. Very few psychiatrists use hypnosis in a group context, though I have had marvelous results with it. I pushed the experiment a step further, using hypnosis with a mixed group.''

"Racially mixed, you mean?"

"Yes, but not only race. Social class, education, age. We have—had—quite a cross-section in the group, and it was amazing how imaginative the members were in questioning each other. I was in the process of writing a paper on it when . . .'' He waved off the bad memory.

"Do you have any tapes of William in this chair?"

"Yes. But of course, I couldn't let you see them."

"Psychotherapist privilege?"

"Yes. I'm sure that William's lawyer wouldn't want anyone else to see them. It might break the circle of confidentiality.''

"I don't recall seeing any mention of a videotape in the police report.''

"I'm sorry?"

"I don't remember the cops mentioning a videotape, William's confession being on tape.''

"Ah, it wasn't."

"Why not?"

"The fact is, he was so agitated when he came in the room, I simply forgot to flick the camera on.'' Again the rueful look. "Possibly the only piece of good fortune William had.''

"Not to be on tape, you mean?"

"Just so."

I stopped for a minute. "I thought you told me a little bit earlier that the reason you spoke to the media about the session was to give William the benefit of an accurate account of what happened."

"That's right," said Marek, darkening a little.

"Well, wouldn't a videotape have been the most accurate source?"

Marek stiffened. "As I told you, I forgot to turn it on."

"All right, Doctor. What can you tell me about Jennifer Creasey?"

He stiffened a little more. "I thought I made it clear that because of potential litiga—"

"Please," I said, interrupting gently. "I just mean simple, nonconfidential things."

"As I started to say, I'm afraid I can't help you there at all. All I know of Jennifer was obtained through professional confidences, either in group or between her and me or William and me." He looked down at his watch.

"Then you saw her privately? Outside the group setting, I mean."

"I'm sorry, Mr. Cuddy, but you'll have to excuse me. I must prepare for my next appointment."

He showed me through the connecting doors into the waiting area. "No further appointments for Mr. Cuddy," he said to Mrs. Porter.

I thanked both of them and left, passing at the threshold an expensively dressed fortyish woman, furtively but intensely scratching herself.

EIGHT

I sat in the car and took out the list of names and addresses
I had copied from the file in Rothenberg's office. One of
the patients lived on a crossway I had passed on the drive
to Marek's building. The patient named Homer Linden.

Linden's place turned out to be a small cape on one of
the lesser streets of Calem, a town that seemed to have
very few lesser streets. The lawn was neat, the shrub-
bery tended but rather sparse. I rang the doorbell. No
answer.

I rang again. Still nothing. Pretty early for someone to
be home from work, and no car in the driveway.

I was reaching for the list again when the door opened.
A man with a shaved head and a drawn face stared out.
He looked about sixty and wore a gray sweatshirt and
running shorts, no socks or shoes. His legs were sinewy
but skinny, and the sweatshirt swam on his torso. I was

yanked back to people I had seen in the cancer ward while visiting Beth.

"Yes?" he said.

"Homer Linden?"

"Yes."

"My name's John Cuddy. I'm investigating the death of Jennifer Creasey. I was wondering if I could talk to you?"

"Sure," he said, "long as you don't mind the stink."

He led me through a small living room and kitchen to an open cellar door. Down the stairs, the basement looked like a combination den, gymnasium, and wet bar, but smelled like all-gym. The fitness apparatus looked home-made and was bunched in a central, space-saving pattern. Floor-to-ceiling bookshelves covered two walls, most holding books but many displaying trophies, plaques, and framed photos. A police scanner radio crackled and squalled once before Linden turned it off. He motioned me toward a bar stool. "Like something to drink?"

"Do you have any beer?"

"Sure do," he said. "I'm a runner, not a teetotaler."

He busied himself at a small refrigerator. I focused on the trophies. Most had a miniature brass-colored man captured in stride.

"Looks like you've been running quite awhile."

"Hah," he said, twisting the cap off a frosty Miller's. "Near to fifty years. Finished third behind John Kelly the second time he took Boston."

Linden passed the bottle to me. I accepted it but paused.

"Go ahead, drink," he said, pulling off the sweatshirt. "I'm only halfway through my routine. Drink and ask your questions."

I thanked him and sipped the beer. He eased down onto a rowing machine as gently as if it were actually a scull at the edge of a dock. He started pulling on the false oars, the muscles appearing magically under his skin as he exerted himself.

"Go ahead, ask away. Don't worry." He grunted. "I ain't gonna die on you."

Homer—"Hell of a name, huh, 'Homer' "—was seventy-four years young. He had retired from the telephone company and decided to become the best runner his age. Marathons, as in 26 miles, 385 yards. The plaques and trophies, smaller in the earlier years, larger as the sport started to catch on, suggested he was nearing his goal. He was one of four older people, three men and a woman, on the cover of a three-year-old *Runner's World*.

"It's funny, most people would figure that the strength goes as you get on, but hell, you see stevedores and butchers and such in their sixties who can still bounce hundred-pound loads around like bean bags. No, it's the flexibility that you lose. 'Less you keep stretching and supporting the joints and so forth."

Linden left the rowing machine for a sit-up board slanted about thirty-five degrees off the horizontal. He straddled the floor end of the board and adjusted a dial. He then edged uphill until he could lock his feet under the bar at the top. Then he edged still higher so that his legs were bent at the knees. He started doing sit-ups.

I stopped talking and drank some beer.

"That can't be all your questions," he said.

"I don't want to wreck your counting."

"Hell, I don't count. That doohickey I set is a timer. I just exercise till it goes off."

I was afraid to ask how long that would be. "How did you come to be in Jennifer's group?"

"Well, after Etta—that was my wife, Etta—after she died, I was pretty depressed. The running and so on helped, but you don't know what it's like to live with somebody for more'n forty years and then lose her.''

I thought I had some idea, but kept quiet about it and swallowed some more beer.

''Anyway, when Etta passed on, a guy I run with, guy about your age, was all hot about this guy Marek and his hypnosis, claimed he'd really brought my friend's mother around after she lost her husband. So I went to see Marek. Didn't much like him at first. My daddy would have called him a snake oil salesman. But the company benefits—old Ma Bell really takes care of her own, don't ever let anybody tell you any different—they covered the cost, so I said, what the hell.''

''Did it help?''

''Yeah, but not so much because of Marek. I mean Marek himself doing any doctoring. The other people in the group were so fouled up, I just started realizing how well off I was.''

A book on the shelf behind him caught my eye. ''That kept you going to the sessions?''

''Yeah, that and . . . well, you wouldn't tell on me, wouldja?''

''Tell what?'' I walked toward the shelf.

''Well, the truth is, I'm not so depressed anymore. I mean, I'm okay now. But the hypnotism stuff is terrific for concentration and relaxation, which you need for training right.''

''And if you weren't being treated for depression, Ma Bell wouldn't pick up the tab for it.''

''That's right.''

I fingered the book. *The Art of Hypnosis* was printed in dark-blue letters on the yellow binding. There were two other books with similar titles around it.

''Looks like you've done a lot of reading on it.''

"Always do. Before I try anything. That's how I built the library. Also how I've stayed alive."

"Marek told me that he uses both drugs and hypnosis."

"He does. On everybody but me, that is. I wouldn't take none of that flurashit if you paid me."

"But he does use it on the others?"

"Oh, yeah. But he shouldn't have been using it on William, neither."

"Why not?"

"Hell, the poor boy was tired most of the time without it, trying to better himself like he was. He looked more worn every week we'd see him."

"Was Jennifer in the group when you joined?"

"Yeah, but not William. He joined later. She brought him into it."

I remembered the police report said there was something between Jennifer and William. "You figure that Jennifer and William were lovers?"

"Huh, 'figure it'? I knew it. Saw them hand in hand, making eyes at each other. Besides, that's mostly what William talked about in group."

"His relationship with Jennifer?"

"More like how it all got started, with the troubles he had at Goreham and all, but you probably know about that, don't you?"

I drew down more of the beer. "Not really."

"Well, it seems, to hear William tell it, that he was discriminated against by some of the students."

"At Goreham? In this day and age?"

"Oh, I don't mean race stuff in a general way. I mean more specifically. One of the white guys there was mad that William took his girl Jennifer away. The guy and his friends made William feel, well, like a colored kid must

61

feel when he knows that some established white kids just can't stand him."

"Do you know the white boy's name?"

"Yeah, but . . . ach, it'll come to me. William and Jennifer both mentioned it. Anyway, William moved home from the school, and I guess that kinda crimped his time with Jennifer, if you know what I mean."

"I take it her parents weren't nuts about him, either."

"That's mild compared to the way she told it. She said her old man—that was the way she said it too: her 'old man'—said her old man woulda killed William if he ever saw them together."

"Funny, I had the impression he was pretty liberal."

"Liberal? Hah, that's a good one. Sam Creasey manages a TV station because his wife's daddy owned most of it. But you ever heard him speak out on things, like I have around town, well, you'd understand why the feds are hassling him about the license. No, Sam Creasey is a very basic kind of man. Like my daddy, only born a hundred years too late. And probably a pretty tough kind of father for a girl like her to have."

" 'A girl like her'?"

"One who'd want to date a colored guy, I mean."

"Did you feel funny opening up in front of the others in the group?"

"Me? No. Not much to tell them." The little binger went off twice, sounding like an oven timer. Linden lay out straight, letting his legs go limp; his feet, still hooked under the bar, kept him from sliding down onto the floor. "It sure was interesting, though, to listen to some of them."

"About the night that—"

"McCatty."

"What?"

"McCatty. Richard McCatty. That was the name of the college kid who razzed William. I told you it'd come to me."

I finished my beer. Linden sat up, gripped the board with each hand near his buttocks, and swung his legs out and down. He stood up, grabbing a towel to wipe his face. "You want another?"

"No, thanks. About the night Jennifer was killed?"

"Yeah?"

"What happened?"

Linden shrugged, tossed the towel perfectly onto a pipe protruding from another piece of apparatus. "Pretty simple, truth to tell." He crouched to reset the timer, then moved to a leg-lifting machine. He sat at the edge of it, wedged his ankles under a pad, and gripped the side of the surface as he had done at the end of the sit-up session. Then he began lifting the pad, and the weights behind him followed on a pulley device. By swinging his feet up, he went from lower legs perpendicular to the floor to legs parallel to the floor. He lowered the weights in twice the time it took to raise them, but didn't continue speaking.

I said, "When did you first arrive that night?"

"About seven-fifteen. I don't have a car, so I usually just bike over so I don't sweat up the place from running. By that time, Lainie and Don were already there."

I thought back to the file. "Lainie Bishop and Donald Ramelli?"

"Right. But Marek said that he hadn't heard from Jennifer or William, so we waited for them. Marek hates to wait, he's a nut on timing, and he was getting pissed. So he shoos the three of us—Lainie, Don, and me—into the session room and we start to decide who should substitute for William in the chair, when he, well, sort of bursts in."

"William?"

"Right."

"He was agitated?"

"And then some. Looking around wild-like, sits down, then jumps up, then sits again. No apologies about being late. Doc goes over to him, shoots him up, and we wait for the drug to calm him down. But it doesn't seem to work. Then the doc begins to hypnotize him anyway—"

"How?"

"How?"

"How does he hypnotize people?"

"Oh, by a little penlight. He darkens the room some, then moves this little penlight back and forth. It's really funny, you know. You say to yourself—you're aware when you're in the chair, aware of what he's doing—and you say to yourself, 'This can't work,' but it does. And then it's so like sleep, you don't remember a thing, any more than you remember a dream once you wake up. Well, anyway, so then Marek asks him—"

"Wait a minute. Marek left the lights down low?"

"No, he turned 'em up again, back at the control panel."

I pictured the room. "Where is that?"

"On the wall, just about at the woodwork. It's hid by the table with the medical stuff on it."

"What's controlled from there?"

"Oh, the lights, the TV camera—he tapes a lot of the sessions."

"What happened next?"

"Let's see. After he brought the lights back up, he started asking William the usual prelim stuff, like William's name, who was in the room, that we're all friends here, and so forth."

"What then?"

"Marek asked William where he'd been, and William

said . . .'' Linden let the weight down and stopped exercising. The binger hadn't sounded. ''William said, 'I just shot Jennifer, the fucking slut bitch. I just shot her in the basement.' '' Linden looked up at me, a sad cast to his eyes.

''We all started to talk at once, but Marek talked over us and said, 'What do you mean, you killed her?' or something like that. And then William just sort of nods and pulls this S and W Detective's Special out and lays it on his lap.''

''How did you know it was a Detective's Special?''

''Huh? Oh, when I was with the telephone company, I carried one. I was an investigator for them.''

''Go on.''

''Well, I got up right away and grabbed the gun. William wasn't really holding it or anything, but I was still scared. I took it, and Marek walked William to the bathroom. William just sat on the john with the lid down while Don and I watched him. Marek and Lainie went downstairs to check. They were back up pretty quick, and Marek said to call the police, but Don already had.''

''Where did Ramelli call them from?''

''From the doctor's office.''

''Ramelli left you alone with William?''

''Sure. I had the gun. Till I gave it to Marek.''

''But it was empty. The police report said so.''

''Yeah, but I didn't know that.''

Yeah, but William would have. And a former investigator who had carried that model should have been able to tell from the weight. Or at least should have swung out the cylinder to check on it. I made an effort not to look back at the hypnosis books.

''What happened next?''

"The cops came pretty fast. They questioned us and took William away."

"William say anything more before the cops arrived?"

"No. Course, none of us were asking him any questions, either."

"Anything else?"

"I don't think so." Linden got off the leg lift and picked up his wipe towel again.

"Nothing else you remember or struck you as odd?"

"No, except for George Bjorkman."

"Bjorkman? One of the cops?"

"Yeah. Him and Clay were the ones first come to the office. I was surprised how he took it."

"What do you mean?"

"Well, George, he was crazy about Jennifer. Wanted to take her to his senior prom in college when she was just a freshman in high school, if you can believe what Jennifer told us in group. Anyway, Sam, her daddy, wouldn't hear of it. I was surprised that George didn't rough William up any, considering what he'd done."

"The killing."

"That and takin' his girl, so to speak." Linden slung the towel around his neck. "More for the takin' maybe than for the killin'."

"Because William was black?"

"Yup."

I asked Linden if I could get back to him in the future, and he said sure, he knew how investigations worked. Linden walked me back upstairs, and we shook hands at his door.

I said, "I really appreciate your time."

"My pleasure, my pleasure. It's good to have someone to talk to, even about something like this." He opened the door for me. "You talking to each of the people in the group?"

"Yes."

"Who else you seen?"

"You're the first."

"Who's next?"

"Any suggestions?"

"Well, Lainie Bishop lives only about half a mile from here. What time you got?"

I looked down. "Five-thirty."

"You should just catch her." He gave me directions to her house.

"Thanks."

"Hope you got a strong zipper," Homer said, chuckling and closing the door behind me.

NINE

Lainie Bishop lived in a development of "estate" homes. You could tell because the private sign beneath her corner's street pole said so. I pulled up to number 18, all the addresses a full six digits apart. Very estatelike.

There was a silver Oldsmobile in the drive. The landscaping looked professional, the house large but without character. The chimes were still bonging when she opened the door.

"Lainie Bishop?"

"Uh-huh," she said, passing the tip of her tongue over her top front teeth. She had dirty-blond hair, cut and fluffed the way Farrah used to wear hers. The face was plain, though her eyes were big, blue, and set wide apart. She wore a pink silk dress that clung in all the right places and ended eight inches above her knees. I guessed her at thirty-five trying hard to look twenty-eight.

"My name is John Cuddy. I'm investigating the death of Jennifer Creasey."

She rolled her head to one side. "What's to investigate?"

"That's what I'm trying to figure out."

"Well, I can't ask you in because I'm on my way out, but"—she rolled her head, curls shaking, to the other side of her shoulders and licked the teeth again—"you're welcome to come with me."

"Sure. Where are we going?"

She turned, stretching back to pick up a handbag. Her hemline rose another four inches. "Cointreau's." She pronounced it "quantrows," like the liqueur.

"What's that?"

She gave me a saucy smile. "My, my. A virgin."

"I guess so."

"C'mon," she said, closing the door behind her. She looked toward the street. "That yours?"

I glanced at my ratty Fiat. "Yes."

"Maybe we better take separate cars anyway. Just in case."

I followed her for three or four miles. We had just entered another ritzy suburb when she wheeled into an immense parking area surrounding a brick and glass restaurant-bar, perhaps two and a half stories tall. There were fifty or sixty cars already there, and five more pulled in as we walked to the door.

"This is Cointreau's?" I said.

"Uh-huh."

The bouncer at the door appeared to be examining the IDs of two guys in front of us. I didn't get it, as they both looked at least mid-to-late twenties. He allowed them in, then waved us past without a word.

"Why the ID challenge for those guys?" I asked Lainie

as we approached closed double doors, muffled music behind them.

"Tonight's over-thirty-only night. They're real strict about it." Then, assertively, "That bouncer's already stopped me a few times."

Uh-huh.

We pushed through the double doors. The music was courtesy of The Byrds. There was a wide parquet dance floor, the largest I'd ever seen in the Boston area. A glitter globe rotated over the twenty or so dancers, flanked by two oblong butcher-block bars with brass rails high and low. Plants with thyroid conditions sprawled everywhere. The only places to sit were high stools around the bar.

"Hey, Lainie, very foxy tonight," said a fortyish guy wearing a print body shirt opened to the navel, a peace medallion, and a gray-black toupee. I checked my watch. Six P.M. If I'd had a calendar, I would have checked the year as well.

"Thanks, Charley," she said.

Charley moved on as three people brushed past us. We headed toward the bar on our right.

Lainie asked me what I was having. Given the name of the place, I ordered a vodka sidecar. When the bartender said, "A what?" I switched to a screwdriver. Lainie ordered the same.

"Well," she said, "what do you think?"

"I'm not sure."

She laughed, edging a little closer as our drinks arrived. "There's a quieter room upstairs. Let me just visit the ladies' room and we can talk up there."

"Fine."

Lainie moved off, her hips swaying provocatively. I felt a hand on my arm.

The hand belonged to a woman with flowers in her hair,

falling long and straight nearly to her waist. She wore strands of love beads around her neck and a sleeveless Grateful Dead T-shirt. Sleeves would have been better, her arms being a little puffier than they were in '68.

"I hope Lainie doesn't think she's bought you with that drink."

"Probably not," I said.

She slid the hand up my arm. "You're in good shape. Aries?"

"No, Reliant K."

She giggled, running her free hand down her hair. "I'm a Pisces. I think we'd be very syncopated."

"I don't syncopate like I used to."

She giggled again. I was making a better first impression than usual. "I have some terrific grass in my car," she said.

"No. Thank you, but no."

She shrugged. "Maybe during another incarnation. Right now, you can call me Bliss." She turned to go. High on her shoulder she had a tattoo of a butterfly that looked as though it was changing back into a caterpillar.

"Forget about her," said Lainie's voice next to me. "She's not your type."

We picked up our drinks and walked toward and up a wide spiral staircase. At the top was a toned-down version of the first floor. Subdued sound system and low glass tables, nubby carpeting and burlaped sectional furniture. Several couples, semi-reclined, already seemed to be getting acquainted. In fact, more than acquainted.

We took a corner piece off by itself. Lainie's dress rode north again as she sat back.

"So," she said, "where would you like to start?"

"What is this place?"

Lainie sipped her drink. "Basically, it's a singles bar."

71

"But the dancing and . . ." I looked around.

"And?"

"And so on. I mean, it's barely six o'clock."

She set her drink down on our little table as The Temptations came on. "Look, the reason for this place is so people, people our age, can come out and feel comfortable. The music and the clothes we grew up with, you know? Most everybody in here has commitments, like kids or responsible jobs or both. So the management keeps out the teenyboppers and gives us a place we can have a good time and still be home by ten." She reached languidly for her drink. "Hopefully, in bed."

I drank, changed the subject. "How did you come to be in Dr. Marek's therapy group?"

She sipped again, then played with her glass. "After my divorce—it was final two years ago—I felt pretty down. This place wasn't open yet, and I didn't like going into Boston. My ex was a real shit. He was a computer whiz at one of the Route 128 companies. You know, home late, sometimes not at all. Running new programs, he said. Why you? I said. He was needed, he said. Why can't somebody else push the buttons? I said. Because he pushed better, he said. Then I found out the buttons he was pushing were on some nineteen-year-old secretary. I got the house, and fortunately my aunt was in the real estate business. The interest rates were coming down, so I refinanced and starting working with her."

"As a broker?"

"Salesman first. Takes a while to get your broker's license." She paused. "You do much divorce work?"

"You mean following husbands for wives, that kind of thing?"

"Yeah."

"No, I don't."

"Too bad."

"I thought you said you were already divorced?"

"Oh, I am, I am. But in my business, well, it's a real help to get referrals. Like if you knew that a couple were busting up, and they had a big house, I could sort of . . ."

"Be the listing broker who helps them sell, for six percent."

"That's right. That's my business. And I'm very good." She lowered her eyelids to half-mast. "At all sorts of things."

I downed more of my screwdriver and asked her again how she came to be in Marek's therapy group.

"My aunt had heard about him. So I gave it a try. The hypnosis stuff is incredible. It drives out all the bad vibes, lets you really relax and relate. At first, I thought the group was pretty . . . well, strange. All different kinds of people with different kinds of problems. But Cliff is very good at bringing people together."

"Like Jennifer and William?"

"Yeah, but Jennifer didn't need much help. She did just fine on her own." Lainie tossed off a third of her drink. "People will tell you she was kind of spoiled, from being rich and all. I never knew her till the group thing, but all she really needed—Oh, just a second, there's somebody I have to talk to. Be right back."

She got up with her drink and quick-stepped over to a slim black man in a conservative three-piece suit. Lainie passed two other males coming our way. One was stocky, with blond hair and a mustache. He looked like the kind of guy who'd buy a BMW with an automatic transmission. The other, taller but skinny, had thinning black hair in a surfer cut. They both swiveled their heads obviously to watch Lainie go by.

"Nice bod," said Mustache to Surfer.

"Nothing face, though," said Surfer.

"You gotta picture her with the lights out," said Mustache.

"You planked her?"

"Not yet, but she's a regular here. Let's just say her next banana won't be her first."

They moved just past me to survey the dance floor from the balustrade of the loft.

"Check the ta-ta's on that brunette," said Mustache.

"White dress?"

"No, red top. The one doing the stress test."

"Oh, yeah. Kind of chunky, though."

"The bigger the cushion, the better the pushin'."

Surfer laughed appreciatively.

"See that one, with the long hair and no sleeves?" said Mustache.

"Yeah."

"I rang her chimes a coupla times. Screwy broad, though."

"How do you mean?"

"Well, her name's Bliss, and she thinks she's still a hippie."

"Boy, a bummer, huh?"

"You ain't heard the half of it. We're in the sack, at her place, her husband's outta town. Well, what they've got is a mattress on the floor, sheets filthy. I don't know how the guy stands it. Anyway, this fuckin' cat hops in with us."

"I hate cats in bed."

"Yeah, me too. So I'm puttin' it to her and this cat hops in and he's only got one ear, like the other one got bit off or something. And she says to it, 'Not now, Vincent,' just like that, like maybe the cat was next after me."

"Vincent?" said Surfer. "That's a funny name to call a cat."

"Yeah, I thought so too," said Mustache.

Surfer looked down to the dance floor again. "What do you think of the two in the corner over there?"

"By that fuckin' whale?"

"Yeah."

"Not bad, but it's still kinda early to pounce yet."

"Yeah, but how about if we check 'em out?"

"Sure, sure. I hate to waste time on a broad I haven't heard talk yet."

They turned away and headed for the staircase. They missed Lainie's approach back to me as The Lovin' Spoonful came through the speakers.

"Sorry about that," she said, settling back onto the sectional. "Terry's wife is bitchin' him up over their joint custody agreement, and it's been tearing at him something fierce."

Her glass was empty. "Let me get this round," I said.

She clamped a hand on my knee. "Already ordered. So where were we?"

She left her hand there. I refocused on the job.

"You were telling me about Jennifer Creasey."

"Right, right. She wasn't a bad kid, really, though she did kind of dazzle poor William. Flashing her WASPy ass at him, you'd think he'd know better. But I guess enough people told him he was smart. And he was too, but smart in the brain sense, not in the mind sense, you know?" Her hand ventured up from my knee a few inches. "Book learning, not worldly wisdom."

The cocktail waitress arrived with our drinks. She carried a tray with eight indentations around the edge, into which the eight filled glasses fit snugly. A truly great invention.

Lainie reached the knee hand up for her drink. A tactical mistake, as I was able to shift my leg away from her. The waitress left.

I said, "Can you tell me what happened that night?"

"Sure," she said, "except for finding her . . . her. I don't want to talk about that."

Lainie related basically the same sequence as Linden had. I thought of a question that I'd forgotten to ask Homer. "Would there have been any reason for Jennifer to see Marek outside the group?"

She clouded up. "What do you mean?"

"Any reason she'd be seeing Marek?" I said as neutrally as possible.

Lainie shook her head, maybe too hard. "No. Cliff . . . Dr. Marek doesn't fool around like that."

I would have liked to pursue the subject, but she seemed sensitive on it, and I wanted other information from her.

"Did you have any reason to think William would harm Jennifer?"

"Nope. Oh, he was wound pretty tight, pressure from the college and Jennifer and all. But I never would have guessed he'd hurt her." She put the accent on the "he'd."

"Who would you have guessed would hurt her?"

She gave me a dreamy look and slid closer, hand to my thigh this time. "I've been thinking. If I answer all your questions now, you won't have any reason to see me again."

"Oh," I said, with the obvious next line: "I wouldn't say that."

She drew her nails firmly across my thigh and leaned over for a kiss.

"I prefer to separate business and pleasure," I said.

"I don't," she said, kissing me on the lips, head moving left to right seductively. I didn't respond.

She pulled back, surprised. "What's the matter, I'm not attractive?"

"I think you're attractive. That doesn't mean I find you attractive."

She lowered her voice. "You're not gay, are you?"

"No, just working."

"Christ," she said. "Whatever happened to Mike Hammer?" She took a drink and looked at her watch simultaneously. "Look, honey, it's been terrific, but I think I'm gonna move on."

"I'd like to ask you a few more questions," I said, she standing and I following.

She gave me the head and curls roll again. "Sure. Sometime when you're not working, huh?" She turned.

"One question, please?" I said.

She sighed. "Okay, one."

"Who would you have bet would hurt Jennifer?"

"Oh, what's his name, the guy she tossed over for William. Richard something. At Goreham. Listening to her, he was a real bastard."

"Thanks."

"Ciao," she said, walking back toward Terry.

I hate wasting a drink, so I downed half my new screwdriver. Which made me look for the men's room. There was one on the second level. When I came out, Lainie was sitting next to Terry, clasping her hands on his and talking very seriously. An image came to me, an image of her consoling a troubled but younger guy like William.

I climbed down the stairs and yielded sideways at the bottom to a couple moving up. I heard Mustache's voice behind me at the bar. "Baby, all I can say is this hombre thinks you are muy beautiful."

I turned my head in time to see Mustache tapping his

chest in front of a chubby woman with the weary face of a nurse working double shifts. Surfer was nowhere in sight.

"In fact," said Mustache, slouching nearer to her, "in the event of a nuclear war, I hope you'd be the last chick on earth."

"Pal" she said, not giving ground, "if I were the last woman on earth, you'd be standing near the end of a very long line."

I walked to the double doors. Simon and Garfunkel clicked on. The baby-boom generation hits middle age. Groovy.

TEN

I turned the key in the Fiat. It wasn't even dark yet. I took out my list and saw that group member Donald Ramelli lived in Wellesley, on my way home. I drove to Wellesley center, got directions from a gas station attendant, and followed them to Ramelli's house.

It was an old wide-bodied ranch on too small a lot. The hedge was scraggly, the lawn rough-cut, with big brown patches. There was a late-model Cadillac sedan in the driveway. However, as I walked to the house, I noticed the left front of the Caddy was staved in. There were also a couple of deep scratches beginning at the driver's door and traveling nearly to the rear fender.

I rang the bell. No answer.

I rang again. From inside the house, a male voice: "Awright, awright. Coming, coming."

The man in the doorway was carrying a tall glass, half

full of clear liquid. He was early forties and medium height, potbellied, in a golfing shirt and Bermuda shorts. His features were thin and red-lined, his still full head of black hair too much for the face it framed.

"Mr. Ramelli?"

"I don't vote, I don't buy, and I don't contribute, even at the office."

It sounded a practiced line, so I laughed. He laughed too.

"I'm John Cuddy, Mr. Ramelli. I'm investigating the shooting in Dr. Marek's building, and I'd like to ask you a few questions."

He rocked back, but pushed open the screen door for me. "Sure, sure, come on in. The Sox are on the tube, downstairs."

We descended to a basement that, unlike Linden's, was mostly bar, a little den, and no gymnasium. A forty-eight-inch projection television was at one end, Jim Rice flexing with a bat. There were water stains on the ceiling and an odor of mildew masked insufficiently by a pine-scented air freshener.

He moved behind the bar. "What'll you have?"

Not "Would you like a drink?" The dented car, sunburst complexion, and opened bottle of vodka on the counter painted a pretty complete picture.

"Screwdriver?"

"Sure." He opened the refrigerator. "Shit, she forgot the o.j. again. How about a vodka tonic?"

"Fine."

He made it quick and strong. No lime. He paused to freshen his. About three ounces' worth. No mixer.

He came back around, gave me the drink. "Sit down, sit down." He gestured toward the TV. "Twi-nighter, to

80

make up for the rainout. The score's already three to one, Oakland.''

I watched Rice send the next pitch towering toward the leftfield wall at Fenway. It caught the screen halfway up. Nobody was on base in front of him.

"Christ, he's something, isn't he? Fucking eight other guys like him, though, they'd still lose ten to nine every game. No pitching. Never had any pitching.''

I remembered Lonborg and Radatz and half a dozen others, but said, "I understand you were there the night Jennifer Creasey was shot?''

"You 'understand'? Aren't you a Calem cop?''

"No, I'm not.''

"Which department you with, then? Not ours.''

"No, no department. I'm a private investigator.'' I dug out my ID. He studied it from several angles, then handed it back.

"Who you workin' for?''

"Willa Daniels, William's mother.''

"Hoo, you'd better be Magnum, P.I., buddy. They got Daniels so wrapped up, Houdini couldn't get out of it.'' He drank from his glass as though it were lemonade. "Poor shit.''

"Did you know William well?''

"Just through the group,'' said Ramelli, answering me but watching the game. "C'mon, Tony. Lose one, lose one.''

"What'd you think of him?''

"Think of him? Shit, that was way outside, Ump, way out. Think of him, huh? Well, I thought he was a pretty good kid who was getting sucked in way past his depth.''

"How do you mean?''

"Well''—drinking—"here he is, a kid who would probably be a top ten percenter in his element, at U Mass, you know, and instead he comes out here and look." Ramelli spread his hands, sloshing a little liquor. He changed hands, licked the wet fingers. "I got nothing against the colored, they never took anything from me, but one look at that Jennifer, and you know old Willie wasn't going to be her one and only, you know?"

"Did she have somebody else on the string?"

"Wouldn't surprise me. She was a real"—he looked at me, trying to gauge something—"she was like a blond-haired Katharine Ross, from *The Graduate,* you know? Refined like that, but a hooker at heart. She had plenty before old Willie, if I'm any judge."

"Do you think she had somebody along with Willie, though?"

"Like I said, wouldn't be surprised. Never saw her with anyone, but you never know with kids these days. Not like us, you know?"

I said I knew. Over the next two innings we covered Ramelli's profession (selling wholesale auto parts) and avocation (watching any sport involving a ball). Regarding the night of the killing, Ramelli was a little fuzzy on certain points, but said nothing to contradict what Homer and Lainie had given me. I didn't bother asking him why he'd joined the group.

I glanced at the set. Jim Rice was back up, which seemed an omen. I stood to leave. Ramelli and his booze escorted me back upstairs.

"Thanks again for the information and the drink."

"Hey, no problem. Sorry about the o.j. Fuckin' Bliss, I don't know where her head's at anymore."

A cat scooted across my path and out of sight. A cat with only one ear.

Ramelli closed the door. I got into my car and out of town as fast as I could find my way.

Between Cointreau's and Ramelli, I was too depressed and tired to drive to Goreham College and hunt for Richard McCatty. He'd be easier to find through a student directory the next morning.

When I got in the apartment, the tape machine's window showed one message. I called my answering service as I rewound the tape. My service said Lieutenant Murphy had called and that I had the number. I thanked the woman and played back the tape. It was Murphy also. "Call me tonight."

I dialed his home number and got a mellow female voice.

"Yes?"

"This is John Cuddy returning Lieutenant Murphy's calls."

"Just a minute, please."

I waited, Murphy came on. "Just a second," he said.

I waited again. "Okay," he said, "what've you got?"

"Lieutenant," I said, as gingerly as possible, "I'm returning your call to be polite, but my client is Willa Daniels, not you. All I'll say is that so far the police report checks out down to the commas."

"Now look, mister—"

"Lieutenant, before we get so mad we can't sleep, let's be straight on what the dispute is. If I find out something, you want me to tell you. I'm saying I won't. Since there's nothing to tell yet, there's nothing to fight about."

He stayed silent. It must have been very hard for him.

"Call me if you need anything," he said in a business-like voice, and rang off.

I stared at the telephone. I wondered why he didn't blow up.

I dialed Mrs. Daniels. I summarized my day for her, and she said she would try to persuade William to talk to me. I told her that Murphy wanted to be kept abreast of what I found out and that my doing so probably couldn't hurt William. She agreed that I could tell him anything I thought could help.

I hung up and thought about calling Nancy, even on a pretext. Instead, I broiled a steak with some canned mushrooms and drank two Molson Golden ales. I carried my landlord's color portable into the bedroom and watched two fires, one robbery scene, and three traffic accidents on the eleven o'clock news before drifting off to sleep.

ELEVEN

I hate waking up to *Sunrise Semester*. I shook the pins-and-needles sensation from my right leg and turned off the set. The clock radio said 6:35 A.M. A little early for investigating.

I did calisthenics for about an hour, including maybe a quarter as many sit-ups on the horizontal as I had watched Homer Linden perform on the slant. Before I went in to shower and shave, I poured milk on a half bowl of granola, which I then put in the fridge. Twenty minutes later, I watched Jane Pauley interview some weather expert about the jet stream while I sat down to breakfast. Granola may be good for you, but even tenderized it's like eating a dirt road.

At eight-thirty, I called the Goreham College general number and got no answer. I fetched my *Times* from downstairs, read for a while, and tried again. After two transfers, I got the student directory operator, who gave me McCatty's dorm address and room telephone. Six rings, no answer.

I next tried Mariah Lopez at U Mass. Somebody's secretary said she would be in by 11:00 A.M. The secretary took my and William's names and gave me brief directions.

I got dressed and first drove down to Boston Garden. I easily found a parking space and walked the three blocks back up to 100 Cambridge Street, one of the state office buildings. The lobby directory listed room 1507 for the Board of Registration in Medicine. Despite Homer's and Lainie's endorsements, Marek's experimental hypnosis therapy still smacked of quackery, and I wanted to check on his background. I took the elevator to the fifteenth floor.

Around two corners I found a powder-blue wall with a reception window cut into it and the board's designation on a silver and black sign. I looked through the window into a multidesked office area. A well-dressed young woman with short dark hair noticed me and smiled brightly. She said, "Can I help you?" as she walked toward me.

"Yes. I'd like to see the file on a doctor."

The smile never wavered. "I'm sorry, but the only information we can give out over the counter is the doctor's current address, alma mater, and graduation and licensing dates."

"How can I get permission to see the rest of the file?"

She half turned and called to another young woman, with shoulder-length blond hair. The colleague came over, echoed the first one's version, and politely suggested that I telephone after 3:00 P.M. to speak with the board's general counsel.

I had a better idea. I thanked them and went back downstairs to the lobby and a pay phone.

I reached Murphy at his office. He said he would see what he could do about getting me a copy of Marek's file. Murphy's voice didn't telegraph any hard feelings from our talk the night before.

I tried McCatty's number at Goreham again. His roommate said McCatty was at an exam and would be back about two. Without identifying myself, I said I'd call back then.

It was only ten-fifteen. Plenty of time to catch Dr. Lopez, then drive to Goreham.

I went back to the car, circled downtown Boston, and picked up Morrissey Boulevard. I passed the sprawling, red-brick *Boston Globe* building on the right and the equally red-bricked but more academic B.C. (for Boston College) High School on the left. Shortly thereafter, the U Mass access road squiggled off toward the water.

The University of Massachusetts is spread over a number of sites. Its main Boston campus is at Columbia Point, a peninsula jutting out into the harbor. The school shares grounds with the John F. Kennedy Library and a huge but abandoned sewage pumping station. From a distance, the U Mass buildings are a monolithic brown, rather foreboding and depressing. Up close, you see that the walls are made of an impossible number of individual, chocolaty bricks, with dark-green windows like polarized sun lenses peeking out well above rock-throwing height.

I parked my car in the indoor garage and climbed to the second floor of the harborside wing. Following my directions further, I found Dr. Lopez's office and knocked. A woman opened the door and smiled at me.

"Dr. Lopez?"

"Yes?"

"I'm John Cuddy. I appreciate your seeing me on such short notice."

"Please come in."

We sat down. Dr. Lopez was fiftyish and slim, with gray curly hair and gold-framed glasses. "I'm told that you're here about William Daniels?"

"That's right."

"Could I see your identification, please?"

I showed her.

"And you're working for William?"

"Working for his mother to help William."

"Last week, I spoke with a Mr. Rothenberg on the telephone," she said.

"That's William's attorney."

"Yes. He didn't mention you."

"I started only two days ago."

"I see."

When she didn't continue, I said, "May I ask you some questions about William?"

She fussed with the collar of her blouse. "We're under a great deal of scrutiny here. At the university, I mean. Are you familiar with us?"

"I know that you try to provide higher education to people of lower means."

Her expression remained neutral. "Nicely put. Our mission is to advance students who wouldn't otherwise have the opportunity to obtain college degrees. Many of them take more than the classic four years. Many eventually finish, most do not."

I said, "And therefore?"

"And therefore our ability, our financial ability to pursue this mission is terribly threatened by . . . by . . ."

"By the legislature seeing one of your best and brightest up on a murder charge?"

She flinched. "Yes."

"That's already happened."

"I beg your pardon?"

"He's already been charged. That damage has been done. Getting him off may not reverse the damage, but his being convicted can only make matters worse."

She paused. "I was under the impression, from the news and Mr. Rothenberg, that there isn't much doubt, any doubt, really, that William shot the girl."

"If that's the case, then your indulging me in a few questions probably can't hurt either the university or William."

The hint of a smile. "I have the feeling, Mr. Cuddy, that you are a very good investigator."

"Not measured by what I know so far. When did you first meet William?"

"When he enrolled here, something over two years ago. Do you need specific dates?"

"No. How did you come to know him?"

"Well, when the students register, they're given information about the variety of services provided here. We call me 'Personal Counseling' to try to take the sting out of seeing a 'headshrinker.' William came to me shortly after he started classes."

"Why?"

She considered that one for ten or fifteen seconds. "I'm not sure I can tell you."

"Patient-psychotherapist privilege?"

"Yes."

"Doctor, given the case against William, my finding out all I can about him is pretty vital. I'm sensitive, even sympathetic, to your position. I wish there were a client-investigator privilege. But frankly, I don't have a lot to go on, and you might tell me something that would help him.''

Lopez played with the blouse again. She made up her mind but talked without looking at me. "William was concerned. He knew he was much brighter than most of the other students here, but he was afraid to show it. Apparently, he'd had some problems with excelling in high school, problems with his classmates there, I mean. So he wanted to be tested by me, to see if he was really good enough to make showing off—that was his expression for it—worthwhile.''

"He wanted to see if he was smart enough to make appearing to be smart worthwhile?''

"Yes. I see you find that surprising. You must remember that many minority children do not enjoy the same family and peer support for educational achievement that majority children receive. For a minority child to excel in schoolwork suggests an alignment of that child with the authority figures in the school. While William's mother appeared supportive, his father was gone, his friends disapproved, and his uncle, a serviceman who probably represented the epitome of aligning with authority, had been killed in Vietnam. Therefore, William was both externally and internally discouraged from displaying his own capabilities.''

"Go on.''

"Well, in response to his request, I gave him all kinds of tests, from . . . Do you care about the names?''

"No, just what you found out.''

"What I found out was that William was one of the most gifted students I have ever read about, much less met. His scores on all sorts of cognitive exercises were virtually off the scale. Though I will deny ever having said this, his going through that high school must have been the equivalent of you or me masquerading at an institution for the severely retarded.''

''Did the test results convince him?''

''Convince him? Oh, yes, he seemed somehow relieved, in fact, as though he'd been told that some extraordinary aspect of him was normal, if not average. Even with the test scores, however, his poor high school grade performance required his, well, 'prepping' here before another, more prestigious college would consider him. His evaluations were superb, and through the help of several of our professors who believed in him, Goreham accepted him as a transfer student.''

''Why Goreham?''

''Because it's a fine school.''

''Granted, but why not Harvard or one of the other Ivies? If he was so extraordinary, I mean.''

Lopez frowned and sighed. ''An Hispanic friend of his went to Harvard, academic scholarship. A black football player to Dartmouth, supposedly academic also but really athletic reasons. Both flunked out their freshman year. One committed . . . well, that's another story. Suffice it to say that William, and I as well, viewed Goreham as both worthy and achievable.''

''Did you stay in touch with him after he transferred there?''

''Not exactly. William seemed to be caught up very quickly in a different world. He . . . perhaps he tried to change too much too soon. Dormitory life, a new girlfriend, the girl he . . . the dead girl, and, well, he had difficulties there.''

''What kind of difficulties?''

''Academic ones. He came here once, midway through his first semester. He showed me some papers he'd written for courses there. C and D grades. The papers had some spelling and grammatical errors, but the professors' written comments focused more on content. William's work, while imaginative, wasn't to the point. He couldn't seem to concentrate his exceptional qualities on the subject assigned. Rather, he took flights, expanding on tangential themes to the exclusion of central ones. It was as though William felt he had to justify their decision in admitting him by blazing new trails in whatever subjects he took.''

"That sounds like a pretty easy difficulty to correct.''

"Yes, but others weren't.''

"Others?''

"Nonacademic ones. Apparently, he suffered some . . . 'hazing' would be the polite word . . . from the boy who used to date the dead girl. Those attitudes drove him out of the dormitory. William had to maintain minimum grades to retain his scholarship, and the commuting from his home to Goreham by public transportation took three hours a day, what with bus and train transfers. Then the social pressures of continuing to see the girl while she . . .''

"Go on.''

Lopez looked squarely at me for the first time since she'd begun talking about William. "I think I have to stop there.''

"Why?''

Lopez just looked at me.

"Doctor, I need to know anything that might help William.''

"This," she said softly, "can only hurt him.''

"Worse than he's hurt already? The authorities have him cold now.''

Her eyes left me, flitted around the desk, then closed. "William was certain that the girl was seeing someone else.''

"Who?''

"He didn't know. It was devastating him. He said . . ."

"Yes?"

She opened her eyes. "He said it made him want to kill her."

We both stopped. I took a deep breath and tried a related topic.

"Dr. Lopez, you knew that the dead girl and William were in a therapy group?"

"Yes, he mentioned it."

"The psychiatrist involved uses hypnosis and a tranquilizer drug called flurazepam to treat—"

"Flurazepam?"

"Yes."

She shook her head. "Mr. Cuddy, I'm fairly certain that flurazepam is a hypnotic, not an anxiolytic."

"I'm sorry?"

"The drug flurazepam. It's more a sleeping potion than a tranquilizer. Using it with hypnosis would be . . . oh, overkill, I would think."

I thought back to Marek and the lab report on William. "How sure of that are you?"

"Well, I'm not a doctor, a medical doctor, that is, and if this psychiatrist, Dr. . . . . ?"

"Marek. Clifford Marek."

"Well, if he's prescribing it, then perhaps my information is out-of-date."

"Is there anyone you could refer me to who might know?"

"You mean, like an expert on drugs?"

"And hypnosis, if that's possible."

"I don't know of anyone. I could make some inquiries and get back to you. If it's important."

"It might be." I gave her my card and home phone.

"Anything else?" she said.

"Just one more question. Off the record, off-off the record, what do you think happened?"

Her eyes welled up a bit. "I think a bunch of well-intentioned people pushed William to the point of shooting someone."

I turned into the driveway and followed it to her part of the hillside. I got out and took the two slanting footpaths to her.

"No flowers this time, kid. I need help."

What's the matter?

"Everybody I've talked to says William did it. Even the people who are supposed to be on his side. Except his mother, of course."

What does she say?

"She says he wouldn't do it, couldn't do it. But it was his gun. And the dead girl was his lover. And four eyewitnesses tell the same story."

What story?

"About William's confession."

Does that make it so?

"How do you mean?" I said, hunching down.

Well, just because he told them he killed her doesn't mean he did it.

"But, Beth, even he says he did it. That was about all he said to me, but even he admits it."

If you're so sure he did it, why are you asking me?

"Because I'm not sure, and that's what bothers me. The young lover confesses under hypnosis. The psychiatrist who does the hypnotizing remembers to dim and up the lights but forgets to turn on a video camera. A patient who's a retired investigator, and who reads a lot about hypnosis, doesn't check a revolver to see if it's loaded. Another patient is a drunk, whose perceptions are therefore suspect. The drunk's wife and another patient play at an overaged-singles bar. Add a college student and a cop who are both ex-flames of the dead girl.''

I don't see the point you're making.

''My point, if it is a point, is that there are loose ends, some of which are probably just coincidence, but all of which, accumulated, seem unlikely.''

Meaning someone's lying?

''Not that I can spot.''

It was silent for a moment. The harbor below was as empty of activity as I was of ideas. Then an Eastern jetliner came in low and deafening over the hill, angling toward Logan Airport at the other end of the harbor.

Basically, she said, *you're troubled that maybe someone else killed the girl.*

''Basically.''

Well, then, if you're at a dead end with William, maybe you should start working on the someone else. If you can't prove William didn't do it, maybe you can prove someone else did.

''Maybe.''

TWELVE

I pulled onto the Goreham campus at 2:15 P.M. I parked in a faculty space and was struck by how empty the grounds were. Then I remembered the roommate's remark about exam time.

I found McCatty's dormitory. A kid wearing an old QUEBEC LIBRE shirt and looking as if he'd just awakened told me McCatty lived on the top floor, ''in that corner''— pointing.

I climbed the stairs. The door in the corner was closed. I knocked on it; no answer. I tried the knob, and it turned easily.

The two guys in the room were stretched out on their respective beds, fully dressed, each with a smoldering toke in his hand. Both wore Walkman headphones, eyes closed, wires running down to a unit on the floor between them. I knocked louder on the open door, but neither acknowledged.

I walked in, sat in one of the desk chairs, and watched them for a few minutes. The smell of the marijuana was strong and sweet. No apparent activity except for draw, hold, and exhale. One was shorter, chubby, in jeans and a Pat Benatar tank top. The other wore shorts and a Ralph Lauren Polo jersey, shirttails out. Polo had the legs of a soccer player, the look of money. I bet myself that Polo was McCatty and that the octopus music machine was his.

I was about to step over when the little floor unit clicked. Polo cursed and said loudly, "Joey, flip it over."

Chubby sat up and nearly didn't see me, jumping when he did. "Who are you?" he said, pushing the earphones back and down so they rode like a necklace.

"John Cuddy. I called earlier. I want to speak with your friend."

Polo cursed again and came up on one elbow. He started to say, "Joey, what the fuck . . ." then saw me. "Who are you?"

"John Cuddy. I'm investigating a matter that you might be able to help me with."

McCatty sank back down into the bed and closed his eyes. "I haven't got time. I got an exam tomorrow. Come back in September." He coughed. "Joey, flip the fuckin' tape, will ya?"

Joey bent toward the tape machine, but kept his eyes on me. I shook my head very slowly, even melodramatically. Joey stopped, swallowed. I hooked my thumb toward the door and mouthed the word "now."

Joey looked to McCatty briefly. I gestured again. Joey took off the headphones, laid them on the floor, and walked out, saying over his shoulder, "Richie, I've gotta see Moon for a while."

"What the . . ." said McCatty, up on both elbows now,

but Joey was already gone. He looked at me. "Get the fuck out of here."

McCatty got up to change the tape. He looked to me again. "I said get out."

"I heard you," I said.

"Well?"

"Why don't we pretend it's intermission at the concert, and you and I are having a nice little talk in the lobby?"

"What about?"

"Jennifer Creasey. I've been hired to look into her death, and I'd like some information."

He'd gotten his back up over the mention of her name. "Get the fuck out of my room."

"As soon as we talk."

"Now!"

"No."

Based on watching him with Joey, I had the feeling little Richard wasn't used to defiance of his orders. It's amazing how readily we mistake one person's acquiescence for the world's obedience. He eyed the telephone.

"I'll call campus security."

"I'd wait till the atmosphere clears a bit," I said.

He looked at his joint, crossed to the desk opposite me, and carefully stubbed it out. He put the stub in a desk drawer. There were actually some books gathering dust on the shelf above it. One caught my eye. A yellow binding with bold blue lettering.

"What's your major, Richard?"

He turned, sneering. "What is this, a mixer? You trying to pick me up?"

I smiled and moved toward him. He took a step back, which put him against the desk. I grabbed his left elbow with my right hand, digging my fingers like nails into the fleshy part.

"Hey," he said, wriggling a little. "Hey, that hurts. Stop it."

I read, sideways, *The Art of Hypnosis* over his shoulder. "What's your major?"

"Psychology. Hey, stop it. No shit, that hurts."

I kept the come-along hold on him and led him back over to his bed. A little push, and he sat heavily as I released the hold. He rubbed his arm, watching my hand.

"You do much hypnotizing in psychology, Richard?"

"Hypnotizing? Yeah, a little. In this seminar, we hypnotized each other."

"When did you first meet Jennifer Creasey?"

"This year. She was a freshman. In September, I met her at a party."

"Date her?"

"Yeah, I dated her." A little belligerence returned to his voice.

"Who broke it off?"

"None of your business."

I shook my head as I had with Joey. Richard got the message.

"She did," he said, head down, "when the black bastard who killed her showed up."

"Daniels lived in this dormitory?"

"Yeah. Single room. You know, special privileges? Shit, you have to be a senior or a cripple or something to have a single. But they gave him one, all right. Make up for his deprived upbringing."

"You welcomed him with open arms, did you?"

"Aw, you don't see it, do you, man? This nigger comes in here, free ride. Free! You know how many cars my father has to sell to pay the tab here for me?"

"No. How do you help him?"

"Help him? Daniels?"

"No, your father. How do you help him pay for all this?"

McCatty wagged his head in disgust. "They think we owe them, and not just a living, either. My father says they think we owe them everything. Food stamps that they cheat on, public housing that they wreck, our schools, our jobs . . ."

"Our girlfriends?"

"Oh, man. You just don't get it at all. Let them rip you off. See if you don't . . ."

"Don't what?"

"Don't get even. Or get them out. Sure, we scared Daniels off. He sucked. Tried to suck up to us when he first got here. That's how he met Jennifer. Here, in this room. He heard some music and came in here. Actually!"

"Imagine that."

"I told him to shag it out. He gave me that mean nigger look, but he went. Moon . . . He went, but no, Ms. Hotpants has to go after him. To apologize. That's how it started with them. Her apologizing for me."

"You going with anyone now?"

He started to give me the belligerent look again, but reconsidered. "No, I'm not."

I got as far as "Where were you the night—" when a powerful arm from behind shot up my armpit and slapped the back of my neck, pushing my head down and my shoulder up and back in a half nelson. The arm was slick and smelly with sweat.

"Moon . . . was in . . . the gym," Joey's voice said. "I had . . . to run." He was out of breath.

McCatty's voice had a satisfied, oily edge to it. "Moon's a wrestler, asshole. Heavyweight."

Moon didn't say anything. I let him get real comfortable with the hold, waiting till he shifted to push me down onto my knees. Then I raised my right foot and brought it down hard just below his knee, using the outside of my heel to scrape the shinbone down to his instep, which I stomped.

Moon released his hold and grabbed for his shin. Without turning, I swung my left elbow up into his left cheek, then duplicated with my right elbow to his right. He teetered from the first shot, went down with the second.

"That's not fair . . ." Moon gasped. He was thick-bodied and hairy, a bear rug in gym shorts. "You can't . . . it's against the rules."

McCatty looked at me with disbelief. Neither he nor Joey spoke.

"The night she was killed," I said, "where were you?"

"Here," McCatty said, then again, "here. In the room. Getting ready for finals."

"That's right," said Joey. "He was here with me. From dinner on."

"Joey," I said, still looking at McCatty, "who are we talking about?"

"Jennifer, right? Jennifer Creasey? Who else we know got killed?"

The alibi, and more important, Joey's voice, had the ring of truth. I stepped over Moon, past Joey, and out.

THIRTEEN

I got back into the car and drove toward Calem. I found the Creasey house, new and modern, but resting on an old farm site. Orchard, small pond, the corner of a stable obscured by the far treeline. Expensive acreage but incongruous, a Beverly Hills mansion dropped into a rural Vermont setting.

The driveway was circular, no cars in sight. I pulled in and walked to the front door. The large brass knocker, a lion's head, was heavy to lift and fell with a sound like a blacksmith's hammer.

A petite woman in a maid's outfit answered the door. In a slight Spanish accent, she said Mrs. Creasey was seeing no one, please. I took out a business card and wrote on the back of it: "For Jennifer's sake, please speak with me." The maid took it, reluctantly, and closed the door.

I waited for five minutes. The door reopened. The maid

said to come in, Mrs. Creasey would see me in the library, please.

The entry foyer was large, the house multileveled, each floor separated by half a dozen steps and overlapping with the floor partially above it. I was led up two levels to a room approximately thirty by thirty, with built-in teak bookshelves and a tasteful arrangement of deep leather furniture. A severe-looking woman, perhaps early forties, stood. She was painfully thin, her high cheekbones prominent in her drawn face. Her right hand held my card, folded lengthwise by the press of her fingers.

"Mr. Cuddy, please sit down. I'm Tyne Creasey. Would you care for any refreshments? A drink?"

I declined and sat.

"Pina, please wait downstairs."

"Yes, ma'am." She left.

"This," said Mrs. Creasey, tossing my card onto the end table next to her, "had better not be some vulgar entrée."

"It isn't, Mrs. Creasey. At least, it's not intended to be. I'm sorry about your daughter."

"Let's spare my feelings, shall we? What did you mean, 'For Jennifer's sake'?"

"Like the card says, I'm a private investigator. I've been hired to look into Jennifer's death."

"Well, since we didn't hire you, I assume you're representing the Daniels boy."

"His mother, actually."

"What does she have to do with Jennifer?"

"Nothing. So far as I can tell, she and your daughter never met."

Mrs. Creasey exhaled elaborately. "Mr. Cuddy, what exactly do you want?"

"I want to see Jennifer's killer arrested, convicted, and punished."

"Admirable. Your sense of civic duty, I mean." Her overall manner somehow made the words seem not cynical. "But why, then, are you working for the Daniels woman?"

"Because I'm not convinced that William Daniels killed your daughter."

Mrs. Creasey started to laugh, then cut it off politely as it rose toward a shriek. She spoke normally. For her. "Sir, I don't mean to question your sanity, but are you aware that four people *heard* him confess? With the gun still in his hand?"

"Yes, I am."

"And you still . . ." She broke eye contact, gave herself a shake that implied I wasn't worth laughing at. A telephone rang downstairs. It stopped before one full ring had sounded. "Perhaps you'd better go," she said.

"Mrs. Creasey, I've answered your questions honestly without interposing any of my own. You've been through a terrible tragedy and therefore I'm here only by your good graces. My sole purpose is to keep another mother from losing her child."

She watched me, reappraising. In a different voice, she asked, "Do you have any evidence that someone other than Daniels killed my daughter?"

"I have oddities, Mrs. Creasey. Jangles. Individuals who didn't act as I would have expected. To find evidence, I need to know Jennifer better. I need you to help me."

"I don't . . ." Her voice quavered, then started again. "I don't know that I can . . . help. Jennifer and I had . . . When she began college, she grew distant. Her father . . . we both were so careful with her. So strict that I . . ." She waved both her hands and lowered her face to them. "Perhaps her roommate could . . ."

I heard the downstairs door open and close, the sound of heavy treading on the stairs.

She looked up, startled. "Mr. Cuddy, I'm sorry, but my husband said—" She broke off, then spoke rapidly. "Deborah Wald, her roommate. She lives in Marion. She left school because of—"

She stopped cold, now staring past me. I swiveled my head around. Two uniformed police officers, one about my age and slight, the other young and beefy, were in the doorway. The young one stomped over to me. "All right, on your feet," he said.

"Officer," began Mrs. Creasey.

"It's all right, ma'am," said the older one, moving in too. "I'm Officer Clay. Your husband called us."

"I said get up." The younger one grabbed my left arm, yanked me halfway out of the chair. I continued up, then twisted my arm back against his thumb, breaking his grip. He reached behind him for the leather sap he probably carried in a back pocket.

"No, George, no need for that," said Clay. Then, to me: "Assume the position against this case here."

I walked around the young one, the name BJORKMAN on the name tag over the badge on his chest. I spread legs and arms, with my hands on the shelf. Clay came up to me.

"Revolver," I said, "holster over my right hip."

Clay tugged my gun out, then stepped back and unloaded it. He put the weapon in one pocket and the bullets in another. He frisked further, my ID and wallet joining the bullets.

"You got a charge?" I asked.

"Shut up," said Bjorkman, moving a step closer.

"Easy, George," said Clay, then, to me: "We'll explain everything at the station."

Mrs. Creasey had her head in her hands. Pina, appearing magically, stood over her. My captors and I walked downstairs and to their cruiser, a third officer taking my keys to follow in my car. I sat in the back of the cruiser with Clay, George driving a bit faster and more recklessly than the situation required.

FOURTEEN

"I said shut up."

I couldn't argue with Bjorkman there. Between the ride in the cruiser and the time we'd sat in probably the only interrogation room in the Calem Police building, he'd told me to shut up ten times minimum.

"Why am I—"

"I said shut up."

"George," said Clay soothingly, "take it easy. Detective O'Boy will be here in a coupla minutes."

I was starting to like Clay. He tried to calm his partner down while giving me an answer that might stop me from riling Bjorkman again. A good cop avoids confrontations; they're rarely productive.

There was a quick rap on the other side of the door. It opened, and a stumpy man in a short-sleeved dress shirt and a polyester tie came in. He had a few long wisps of red hair on the top of his head and a fringe of short-cropped fuzz around his ears. He juggled a manila file folder and what looked like my gun, wallet, and ID.

"I'm Detective Paul O'Boy," he said to me. He asked Clay, "He been read his rights?"

Clay nodded, looking tired.

O'Boy turned back to me. "I'm in charge of the Creasey girl's murder. You were out bothering her mother today. Why?"

I said to Bjorkman, "Gee, Georgie, aren't you going to tell him to shut up too?"

O'Boy said, "What are you talking about?"

"Officer Bjorkman here has been telling me to shut up for half an hour now. I thought it was because I was asking him 'why'-type questions. Now I'm not so sure."

O'Boy said, "Why don't we cut the shit and answer my question?"

I looked at O'Boy and said, "William Daniels's mother hired me to help his attorney investigate the murder. I wanted to find out about the girl's background."

Bjorkman snapped at me: "Whaddya mean, her 'background'?"

"Oh, just little things. Like who she was dating, who she threw over. Things like that, Babyfat."

Bjorkman came off the edge of the table, hands balled into fists. Clay clamped his arms from behind and pulled him back to the door. Very quick and very strong, Clay, nice adjuncts to his brains and manner. And Homer seemed on target regarding Bjorkman's feelings for Jennifer.

O'Boy said, "Take him out of here, Clay. Then you come back."

Bjorkman was seething as Clay squeezed him through the door and O'Boy kicked it shut behind them.

"Well," said O'Boy, "you got that all out of your system now?"

"You know, you're going to have trouble with Bjorkman. If you haven't already."

"Let's talk about you. You say you're investigating the murder. Terrific. It's the best case I've ever seen. Set in concrete. But everybody's gotta make a living, right? So you're on a per diem and you don't wanna miss tomorrow's bread ration. Fine. Talk to anybody you want. Me, the chief, the governor. Just stay off the Creaseys, okay? They already had enough about the daughter."

"Mrs. Creasey wasn't all that upset by me. Why the cruiser?"

"The maid called the husband. He called us. Miracle he got through, our phones've been on the blink."

"Your name was on the homicide report as investigating officer, right?"

"Right."

"Anything strike you as odd when you got there?"

"Odd?" said O'Boy, his voice rising. "Odd? No, of course not. We get hypnotized kids confessing to shooting their girlfriends alla time. Used to be one a week."

"Strike you as odd that Marek never turned on the video equipment?"

"He forgot."

"He remembered to dim and up the lights for the hypnosis."

"Heat of the moment. You do funny things."

"Focus on Daniels, then. You just shot your girlfriend. First thing you do is keep an appointment with your shrink?"

"Kid was there, in the building already."

"And submits himself to hypnosis, when he knows he'll tell the truth about it?"

"The kid was screwed up. Pressure from school and shit. Who can say what he was thinking? Maybe he figured confession'd be good for the soul."

"So what's his motive?"

"For killing her?"

"Yeah."

"For chrissake, he was a black kid out of his league, fucking a rich white chick. Maybe she wouldn't blow him and he got peeved. Who am I to say?"

"I heard Bjorkman used to date her."

O'Boy hardened a little. "You heard wrong."

"Something about a senior prom?"

"The fuck do I know? I look like I was his guidance counselor or something?"

"They teach hypnosis at the police academy?"

"Used to. Then with—Hey, what're you getting at?"

Clay came back in. "Bjorkman's in the locker room. He'll be okay."

O'Boy said, "Mr. Cuddy's just leaving. How about you escort him to his car."

"Fine," said Clay, taking my gun and things from O'Boy. "I'll give these back to you at the car."

Clay and I walked side by side out to the parking lot. When he got to my car, he handed me my stuff, keys included, but bullets separate from gun.

Clay said, "You shouldn't have ridden George like that."

"He was behaving like an asshole. In the MPs, if one of my troopers ever put on a show like that, he'd be doing push-ups till his arms fell off."

"George really felt for the girl. You knew that when

110

you goaded him. By the way, he was with me all that afternoon, four o'clock on till we got the call.''

I wondered how long Clay had been listening outside the interrogation room door, but I said, ''Then you and Bjorkman responded to the murder scene, right?''

''Right.''

''Anything strike you as odd?''

''Yeah, one thing.''

''What?''

''That you think I'll give you something after you called my partner 'Babyfat.' Have a nice day.'' Clay turned and walked away.

More impressive all the time. Except for volunteering an alibi for George.

I reloaded my revolver and holstered it. I started the car and pulled slowly to the exit driveway. A midnight-blue Mercedes, the biggest one they sell, screeched on its way in and cut me off.

A tall man in a gray suit got out from behind the wheel, slamming the door behind him. He was about forty-five and could have been Gregory Peck's younger brother. He strode determinedly to my car window and said, ''Are you John Cuddy?''

''Yes.''

''I'm Sam Creasey. I want to speak with you about bothering my wife. In my car.'' He turned and strode back to the Mercedes and got in.

I didn't move.

He reopened his door and, half emerging, curved his torso around the frame to yell at me. ''I'm waiting.''

I didn't answer him.

He came all the way out, slamming the door harder this time. About halfway to me, however, his stride faltered, and he walked very slowly the last few feet.

"We . . . my wife and I have been under incredible pressure the last few weeks. We . . ."

"Look, Mr. Creasey, I had nothing to do with the pressure, but you had me hauled out of your house and dragged down here. Now, if you want to talk, we'll talk. Why not move your car out of the way and climb in? I'll drive us around for a while."

FIFTEEN

"So how did you know it was me?" I said.

Creasey looked at me blankly from the passenger seat.

"Back there at the police lot. How did you know it was me you were blocking in?"

"Oh, Pina—our maid—described you and . . . and your car."

I turned left onto a nice country lane and hoped the split seams in the old Fiat's upholstery weren't razoring his suit.

"Mr. Creasey, I am truly sorry about your daughter's death. . . ."

"Why can't you just leave us alone?"

"Because I've been retained to investigate her killing."

"What can there possibly be to investigate? He had the gun, he confessed before witnesses. He killed her, and he should hang for it." There was just a trace of a southwest accent in Creasey's voice.

"Are you from around here originally?"

"What?"

"Did you grow up here?"

"No, no. Texas. My father owned a spread near Fort Worth. I came east to school."

"Where you met your wife?"

"That's right. They used to have ice cream parties at Wellesley on Sunday afternoons and invite the Harvard . . ."

I glanced at him, but he didn't continue. "What's the matter?"

"I don't usually open up like that. Where did you learn your interrogation technique?"

"Military police for a while, insurance investigation afterwards."

"Combat?"

"Some."

"Vietnam?"

"I was a little young for Korea."

"I was in the Dominican Republic. Marines, OCS navy program."

"You trying to open me up, Mr. Creasey?"

Almost a smile. "No, I was just thinking how much Tyne's family was against my being in the marines. An infantry platoon leader instead of a corporate executive." He blew out a breath. "Simpler times, in so many ways."

"You get older, life gets more complicated."

"No, it was the times. The choices were so much easier then. Clearer, more like my father's days. If he caught a man cutting some of our stock—I'm sorry, you'd call it 'rustling,' I guess—there wouldn't be any drawn-out litigation. The cattlemen would just take care of it."

"How do you mean?"

"Well, the war—Second World War—was on, so most of the younger men were in the service, and there never were many peace officers anyway, so the ranchers just resolved it. If the man had been cutting to feed his family, he'd have to work it off for the spread he'd stolen from."

"What if he was cutting for profit?"

"Then something else'd happen."

"A little more severe?"

"A lot more severe. You were in combat. You catch some little shit you know did one of your men, but he isn't worth a nickel to intelligence . . . I mean, you could just look at him and know nobody'd trust him with any bigger secret than how to pull a pin from a grenade. Does the line platoon feed him, wash him, and escort him back to the rear?"

I didn't like the memories Creasey was stirring for me. The country lane ended at a T-intersection, and I turned right.

"How did you get into television?" I said.

"Tyne's father got a license for one of the first stations up here in the early fifties. He had a manager who brought it along for about fifteen years. When I was finishing my hitch, it seemed a good place to start. The manager died within a year, and I took over."

"Are you happy with it?"

Creasey laughed, then said, "Sorry. It's just that your question reminded me of an interview I had at Harvard my senior year. Tyne and I were engaged, and I was already committed to the marines, but Tyne's father insisted I interview with this corporation that one of his college friends owned. So I'd have 'options' when I got released. Tyne's father was big on options. I met with some junior executive from the corporation, and what was scary was that he really resembled me. We both wore suits, obviously, but I mean his features, hair color, build, all like a ten-year-older version of me. Within five minutes I couldn't stand the guy. He had a bow tie and couldn't talk about anything but the corporation, and his responsibilities, and the long hours. I guess he was pretty much turning off on me too. At one point, maybe fifteen minutes into the interview, he looked at his watch, actually tapped it with the index finger of his other hand, and he asked me if I had any more questions. I said, 'Just one. Are you happy?' Just like that. 'Are you happy?' Well, he stared at me, and I was fairly certain he was trying to decide what 'relevant' question I could have asked that would have sounded like 'Are you happy?' Then he cleared his throat, said yes, he was, and we stood and shook manfully. I laughed all the way home.''

"And I remind you of that guy?"

"No, no. I was just thinking that I am happy. At the station, I mean. It's a responsible, fulfilling job. I know it sounds like a reprise from *Camelot*, but the fact is that I get to do the things I want to do, the sort of programming I believe is important. That's what makes this license renewal so . . . I'm sorry, that's not your problem. Anyway, the station, the job, has made the rest of . . . this almost bearable.''

While Creasey was talking, I tried to watch as continuously as I could without crashing the car. I was ready to despise him after the scene at the police lot, but there was something about him that was straight and true. Like the roles Gregory Peck himself used to play.

"Mr. Creasey, I'm sorry to drag you back to your daughter's death, but is there anyone who hated her or could have benefited in some way from her death?"

He didn't answer right away. "You really do your job, don't you, Mr. Cuddy."

"I'd be more comfortable with just 'John.' "

"And me with 'Sam,' " extending his hand. We shook. "Is there anyone?"

"Hard for me to say. Jennifer led her own life. A little too crazily, even for today's world. There was a fellow at college whom she jilted for the Daniels boy. . . . "

"Richard McCatty."

"Yes. I understand he hated both Jennifer and Daniels for it. So did George Bjorkman. Incidentally, that was why I was coming to the police station. To confront the chief for sending Bjorkman to my house. I just saw you and got diverted."

"Why did that upset you? Bjorkman, I mean."

"When Bjorkman was in college, he wanted Jennifer to go to his senior prom. She was only a high school freshman, for God sakes, so I wouldn't allow it. She wanted to go, too, not for Bjorkman but just to see what that kind of event would be like. She liked to . . . experiment, Jennifer. Well, Bjorkman kept hanging around our house, and I finally threw him out."

"Physically?"

"Yes. He's big, but . . . well, you've seen him."

"I know what you mean."

"Anyway, he resented it. Can't blame him for that, but he somehow got it into his head that I had poisoned Jennifer against him, ruined a romance that would otherwise have been perfect. Crazy, but I'm sure he's never forgotten it."

"Seems odd that he could get on the force. I mean, with you probably having enough reason and influence to keep him off."

"I don't think you understand how things work here."

"Can you explain them to me?"

"Well, I have a certain amount of influence because of Tyne's money and my position. But when you run a television station, you make a lot of enemies too. Not just the ones after the license, either. Even had a crackpot take a shot at me a few years ago. And our editorial policy hasn't always put Chief Wooten and the department here in the best light."

"Still . . ."

"You haven't met the chief yet?"

"No, just Clay, Bjorkman, and O'Boy."

"That's part of what I mean. Paul O'Boy is a good detective, but wouldn't you think the chief himself would have warned you off, given your impression of my importance?"

"I guess I should have, but I didn't think of it at the time."

"Well, that's Wooten's way of telling me where I rank with him in an uncriticizable way. His department has to respond to me immediately, but he doesn't have to do it personally."

"And that's why Bjorkman got on the force?"

"No, that's why I couldn't keep him off. Bjorkman got on the force because he's the nephew of the mayor's wife. The chief sent him to my house just to tweak me."

"Sam, did anybody beyond McCatty and Bjorkman have any reason to hurt Jennifer?"

Creasey passed his right hand over his face, massaging around his eyes. His voice sank below a conversational level. "I've just never thought about it. With all the evidence pointing to the Daniels boy killing her in some kind of rage, it never occurred to me that someone would have . . . could have set it all up."

He stopped, appearing exhausted. I said, "Will this next right take us back to the police lot?"

"Yes. Less than a mile."

We rode in silence till I pulled in next to his Mercedes. He opened my passenger door, then hesitated.

"John, I really loved my daughter, despite some of the things she did. Do you think there's any chance that the Daniels boy didn't kill her?"

"So far, all I have are some facts that don't look right in context. A couple of inconsistencies. Nothing that would persuade a jury."

"Who said anything about a jury?"

He got out and closed the door.

SIXTEEN

I eased out of the police lot into a bottleneck of rush-hour traffic. Rather than battle it, I found a small Italian restaurant at the edge of the town center and parked in a slanted spot next to it. The decor was tacky, and there were plenty of empty tables. I decided to try it anyway. I should have chosen the traffic.

Forty-five minutes later I was back in my Fiat and heading toward Boston. I pulled into the space behind the condominium building that went along with my rented unit, and got out. A voice from a car parked in a metered space called my name softly. I looked over. It was Murphy, in an unmarked sedan.

"Waiting long, Lieutenant?" I said, walking toward him.

"Called you three times."

"I didn't get any messages."

"I didn't leave any."

I glanced toward my building. "Want to come up?"

Murphy seemed unsure of himself. Except for the time when he'd come to my office, I'd never seen him that way. I doubt anyone after his third grade teacher ever had.

"Might be better," he said.

"Beer?"

He said, "No . . . Yeah, if you're having one."

I crossed to the kitchen, motioning Murphy to my landlord's couch. He settled into the cushions, looking around.

"It's rented," I said. "Furnished."

"Didn't figure you had much left. From the fire and all."

I saved him a decision on whether to have his Molson's in a glass by taking out one of the frosted Danish mugs that my landlord had assured me were freezer and dishwasher safe. I poured the beers, the inside liner of ice floating to the top like sleet on a pond.

He thanked me for the beer and took a long draw. He set it on the glass-topped coffee table and coaxed a thick business-size envelope from his inside jacket pocket.

"I got the information on William's psychiatrist for you."

I took the envelope from him and opened it. There were Xeroxes of a bunch of forms, typed in. They appeared to be Marek's completed application for licensure from the Board of Registration in Medicine.

"Be best if nobody else saw those," said Murphy, taking another drink.

I set the forms on the table. They made a crackling sound as they refolded themselves. "I'll go through them later."

We stared at each other for a moment. Murphy fidgeted on the couch. "You got a question, ask it," he said.

"I'm wondering why you didn't leave a message, telling me to come by your office to pick these up."

"Not supposed to have the forms in the first place. Wouldn't look too good for your answering service to know about them."

"You could have left a blind message. Just to call you or stop by headquarters."

"Could have."

"Instead, you cool your heels in front of my place for, what, an hour?"

"Closer to two."

"Anything you want to tell me?"

"About what?"

"About why you're giving so much personal attention to a case you asked me to look into as a favor to an old girlfriend?"

Murphy just watched me.

"For her son, whom you saw, if I remember correctly, once about ten years ago in a store?"

Murphy picked up his beer, took a small sip, looked over the rim at me, and took a three-gulp slug.

"You were married once, right?" he said.

"That's right."

"You always stay straight with her?"

"Yes."

"You never fooled around?"

"No."

Murphy gave me a skeptical look.

"My wife and I were close. Always. She died before . . ."

"Before what?"

"I don't know. Before I thought about it, I guess. She was just the only one."

Murphy blinked. "The only one? Like ever, you mean?"

"That's right."

Murphy shook his head. "You really are one of a kind, Cuddy." He said it without sarcasm.

"You and Willa Daniels, huh?"

"Yeah. Gayle and me were married maybe three years. We wanted kids, but it wasn't happening, so we went for one of those tests. We went twice, actually. Doctor said it was Gayle. She just couldn't conceive. We tried all kinds of—"

He stopped. I began, "You don't have to—" but he cut me off.

"Look, you wanted to hear it, right?"

"Yes."

"You kept asking about it, right?"

"Right."

"Okay. So let me tell it." He took a breath and continued. "We tried a lot of things. Taking temperatures, scheduling making love. All for a kid. But there was something about the scheduling, the arranging of it, that took away the enjoyment of it. The feeling of it, between her and me. Especially when it wasn't working, when she still couldn't conceive. So . . ." Murphy finished his beer.

"Want another one?"

He declined. "So I met Willa. She was working in an insurance agency. Somebody at the agent's home office thought maybe he was padding claims for one of his insureds, who seemed to have a lot of costly burglaries. I was still in uniform then, but they put me in plainclothes for a morning and lent me to Burglary to interview the guy's black secretary. That's how it was done in those days.''

"She married then?''

"Yeah, but her husband was already a shit. Dog track, losing the rent money and spending what he won on booze and white hookers. Willa didn't believe in divorce.''

"Divorce? You were that serious about her?''

Murphy looked puzzled, then spoke quickly. "No, no. I didn't mean divorce so she could marry me. With Gayle and me, it was just . . . well, it was like a time when it wasn't working right after it had been great for three years. I just couldn't see past the period we were going through. It seemed like it was a time that was going to go on forever.''

"You started seeing Willa then?''

"I suppose so.'' He shrugged. "At first, we just had lunch. I'd make up an excuse, that I had to see a guy about this case or that one. Willa would meet me at a restaurant. She was afraid her boss—who turned out to be straight on the claims, by the way; we didn't bust him—that her boss would suspect something if I came by to see her at work. Willa's husband was a little free with his hands, and one lunch she had a bruise under her eye. I had a talk with the shit after he got off what little work he did one day. He left her alone after that. Completely alone.''

Murphy diddled with his mug. "I'll take that other beer, if it's still okay?''

I went to the fridge and popped another bottle for him. I'd barely touched mine. I came back in and handed him the beer.

"Thanks.'' He poured half of the beer, and drank half of what he'd poured.

"Anyway,'' he said, "Willa was a damned attractive woman then, and her husband was a bastard, and I was feeling, I dunno, like I wanted to fall in love again, I guess. And so we went at it."

"Long time?"

"Two, two and a half months. More like therapy than romance, actually. We had to schedule things, like Gayle and me, only . . . only it was different. We were really helping each other, I think. To grow up."

"What caused it to end?"

"Willa. Willa getting pregnant, I mean. She and I were always real careful. As careful as you could be back then. But one night her husband came home drunk, and some pross had shorted him, and, well, he . . . took it out on Willa, without any precautions. I don't know whether it was him or me. But Willa wouldn't have an abortion, wouldn't hear of it. And her being pregnant changed the other thing we had." Murphy sipped some more beer. "So we stopped seeing each other, pretty much stopped even talking with each other. Then William came along, and her husband got even shittier, and eventually left. I couldn't help her much; her parents pretty much took her in. Then, with everything else in life, I sort of lost track of her and William."

I drank some of my beer. It was getting warm, but I wanted something to do.

Murphy stopped, poured off the rest of his second into the mug. "So now you know."

"Dr. Lopez, William's counselor at U Mass, and Willa talked about William's getting a free ride at Goreham. Were you helping out there?"

"A little. William wanted to live in the dormitory, like a real college kid, not a day-hopper. Willa was a little short, so I . . . We can borrow some against our pension."

"Pretty good alternative investment."

"Oh, yeah," said Murphy, tossing off the last of his beer. "Thanks to me, William got to meet the girl they say he killed. Terrific investment."

"I'm not so sure he killed her."

"You got proof?"

I summarized for him the discrepancies I'd spotted so far.

Murphy mulled them, then said, "If I weren't emotionally involved in all this, I'd say you haven't got squat."

"I'd like to keep looking."

"I spoke to Willa about William not helping you. She said she talked to him and he agreed to see you again."

"I'll go tomorrow."

Murphy got up, walked to the door.

"Lieutenant?"

"Yeah?"

"Am I the first person you've talked with about you and Willa?"

Murphy half turned, then threw back the dead bolt to leave. "You know your problem, Cuddy? You always ask one question too many."

It was as good an answer as any.

I called Willa Daniels and brought her up-to-date on the investigation, with the exception of the confessional with Murphy. She thanked me warmly for the small optimism I let her feel.

Next I dialed Information and got the number of the only Wald family in Marion. The operator even asked me if I didn't mean Wall or Walsh. I thanked her and tried the number.

A woman answered on the second ring. "Hello?"

"Mrs. Wald?"

"Yes."

"Do you have a daughter named Deborah Wald?"

"Yes. Who is this, please? Is Debbie all right?"

"My name is John Cuddy, Mrs. Wald. I'm a detective looking into the murder of Debbie's roommate, Jennifer Creasey."

Mrs. Wald's voice dropped. "I thought that was all over with."

"I'm afraid not."

"Well, Debbie isn't here right now. She's out with friends." A different tone crept into her voice. "I don't think she'd be of much help to the police anyway."

Sometimes you get further by not correcting a misimpression. "Even so, Mrs. Wald, I'd like to talk with her."

She paused. "Well, Debbie works breakfast and lunch at the country club restaurant. She'll be home tomorrow after two-thirty or so."

"That should be fine. Can you give me some directions?"

Mrs. Wald dictated a long series of turns, rotaries, and ill-marked roads. She said it was about an hour and a half from Boston.

"Given the distance, Mrs. Wald, are you pretty sure that Debbie will be home then?"

"Oh, yes. She has to be. They're . . ." Her voice cracked. "They're taking the piano away tomorrow." She started to cry and hung up.

SEVENTEEN

Having gone to bed unnaturally early, I woke up unnaturally early the next morning. By 6:00 A.M., I was ready to run.

I crossed Beacon Street and over the footbridge, only two or three cars passing on the usually clogged Storrow Drive beneath me. I turned left and moved upriver.

The banks of the Charles are eerie at dawn. The ghost of a full moon, looking embarrassed to be still visible, stares down upon homeless men and women. They sleep on hard slatted benches, wrapped cocoon-like in stained blankets against the damp air. Four or five push shopping carts full of cans and bottles, rummaging through trash barrels and abandoned paper bags to collect enough returnables for the day's food or drink. Interspersed are the severely mentally disturbed, also without shelter following the wholesale release of the supposedly harmless ones from the Commonwealth's institutions. They meander slowly and mutter, or march like storm troopers and shout, their strings of obscenities provoked by inner, private devils. Toss in fifteen or twenty fitness-conscious, fast-lane urbanites who sweat and swerve along the macadam running paths, wearing designer jogging outfits and "Have a nice day" smiles for each other. Hieronymus Bosch was born five hundred years too soon.

I got back to my place and cleaned up. Making a ham sandwich for breakfast, I settled down with the papers on Marek that Murphy had given me the previous evening.

I riffled through the forms, then organized them into what appeared to be a rational order. The first was an Application for Endorsement Registration. It had been filed only two years and eight months before, which surprised me a little. Marek was a lot more recently admitted to practice in Massachusetts than I would have guessed. Maybe his furniture really was rented.

The application requested, and Marek had provided, premedical, medical, and postmedical schooling, together with hospital appointments. He had gone to school in California, with subsequent hospital positions in New York City, Philadelphia, and finally Chicago, before coming to Massachusetts. Marek apparently had never been certified by any specialty board.

Next on the application was a list of fourteen questions, asking roughly the medical equivalent of "Are you now, or have you ever been, a member of the Communist party?" They included whether his license had ever been revoked, whether he had ever failed a state exam, and whether he had ever been censured or dismissed by a hospital. Marek naturally had answered each of them "No."

The next page of the application contained a completed verification of medical instruction and graduation from the dean of Marek's medical school, along with a photograph of a younger, thinner-faced Marek. Apparently our climate was agreeing with him. There followed a certificate from a Dr. Jerome Gemelman, at the hospital in Chicago, that Marek was of good moral and professional character. Finally, there was an affidavit of the secretary of the Illinois medical association that Marek was duly licensed there, with attached Xeroxes of certificates from Pennsylvania and New York.

The second document was an application for a FLEX endorsement, which seemed to deal with some kind of standardized test. The form called for, and received, the same information in the same order as the initial application for registration.

Read in the context of the rest of the documents, it seemed that Marek, having received a high enough score on the FLEX test and having been licensed elsewhere and vouched for personally, was pretty much automatically granted a license to practice here. There was also a pro forma application for renewal from Marek and an approval of the renewal of his license. I pulled a sheet of blank paper from a desk drawer and made some notes. Then I slipped the documents into a manila folder and put them into the drawer. I dressed in a coat and tie and went down to the car.

William didn't look any happier to see me this time. The guard who brought him took up his same position and watched William carefully.

"Hi, William," I said. Involuntarily, I found myself examining his face for any surface resemblance to Murphy. I saw none.

"Look, my mother wants me to talk to you, I'll talk. For her. But you and me ain't friends, so let's just get on with it, okay?"

"Whatever way you want it to be."

"That's how it is. What I want don't matter." He paused. "Never has."

I started by listing the people and steps I'd pursued so far. When I finished, William snorted derisively.

"That Murphy must have you on the hook real bad for you to blow so much time on this thing."

"Maybe I'm beginning to believe that all this didn't go down quite like everyone says."

"You wanna be thick, that's your business. Ask me your questions."

"How did you meet Jennifer?"

William made a face, but started answering. "When I got to school—Goreham, I mean—I met her one day in the dorm."

"In Richard McCatty's room?"

"Yeah. Him and some of his goon friends were there too."

"McCatty give you a hard time?"

"Oh, no," said William, exaggerating the words. "He didn't give me no trouble. He the soul of integration, the motherfucker."

"When did you start seeing Jennifer?"

"She come out to apologize for McCatty's attitude. She come on real nice, asked me to have coffee with her."

"Did you?"

"Yeah. We went to the student center and talked."

"How long?"

"Coupla hours. What the hell does this have to do with anything?"

"Probably nothing, but I have to get a sense of how things came along."

" 'How things came along'? What the hell you think came along?"

"What do you mean?"

"She did me, man. She took me back to her room after the coffee and all and she did me."

"Sex."

"No, mother'. Body painting. Shit, of course sex. Blow job. Said it was her period."

I stopped for a minute. William looked at me reproachfully. He said, "That all your questions?"

"No. I was just thinking."

"What?"

"Just that everybody I've talked to implied that you and she were serious. As in romantically serious."

William laughed. I took a chance. "William, you're the first one who's suggested she was just a convenient piece of ass."

He got angry, then tried to cover it. "People don't know what the fuck they're talking about. You shoulda learned that by now."

"Was Jennifer seeing other guys while she was seeing you?"

"You mean was she fucking other guys, don't you?"

"That's what I mean."

"Probably. Yeah, definitely. She liked to fuck."

"Who?"

"Who she fucked?"

"Yeah."

"I don't know." He laughed again, short and bitter. "Tell you what—you bring me a student directory, maybe a faculty directory too, and I'll underline the definites and check off the probables."

"Let's talk about Dr. Marek. How did you come to see him?"

"Jennifer's idea. She was in this group, thought it might be good for me."

"Was it?"

"Yeah, terrific," he said, exaggerating again and sweeping his head around the room. "Given me a whole new perspective on my existence."

"Was it doing you any good before Jennifer was killed?"

William exhaled, ran his hand down over his eyes quickly. "Look, I was fucked up. I was in over my head, you dig? I went from the street to U Mass to big time in like months. I know it reads years on the calendar, but not to me. I was dizzy, man. You got no idea. It was like watching television all your life, being envious of what you saw, then all of a sudden starring in your own show. Having people focus on you, evaluate you without you knowing what the measure was they were using. You know what it's like to have the people at U Mass tell you you're a fucking genius, then hit a place like Goreham and realize that genius is a real relative thing?"

"So did Marek help with any of this?"

"I dunno. The hypnosis stuff, yeah, I think that did me some good. In the beginning anyway. Then . . ."

"Go ahead."

"Forget it, man."

"William, what were you going—"

"I said drop it, man! Or I'm fucking finished talking with you."

"Okay." I made a mental note to come back to it. "Did you get to know any of the other members of the group well?"

"You shitting me? You talked to them, right? They

133

were more fucked up than I was. Lainie was a slut, Ramelli was married to one, and Homer, I think he was in for some kind of weird training reason. Like it made the old fuck a better runner to listen to us nuts crack open once a week.''

"How about Marek himself?"

"He was crazy too. He'd have to be, to put up with the rest of us.''

"How else did he strike you?"

"He's a headshrinker. He makes his money like a hooker, charging for his time to make you feel better.''

"You think Jennifer and Marek ever made love?"

William's anger flicked on again. "The fuck do I know?''

"You were pretty close to her, and you must have seen her with him before, during, and after group. That sounds like enough basis for an opinion.''

He grew angrier. "You wanna know, I'll give you my 'opinion.' My opinion is that you like to ask about fucking sex more than you like to have it.''

I took a deep breath, let it out. "Before Jennifer was killed, how were you and she getting along?"

William looked down, anger draining. "Fine, just fine.''

"No arguments, splits, anything like that?"

"I said no. We were *fine*. We *fucked* fine. All right?''

"You know a cop named Bjorkman?"

"Oh, yeah. Another great friend of the Negro.''

"He harass you?"

"You could call it that.''

"Any specific instances?"

"Yeah, plenty. Jenn and me would be walking, and him and his partner would pull up in their police machine and tell us stories.''

"Stories?"

"Yeah, about how little nigger boys that bother with little white girls end up as fertilizer back in the woods somewhere."

"Both Bjorkman and Clay said things like that?"

William thought for a second. "No, to be honest, I only remember the partner being there once, and he came down on Bjorkman and made him drive the car away. Bjorkman, though, he'd sometimes wait outside Marek's building and ride me, or just watch me when I'd get there."

"Was he there the night Jennifer was killed?"

"I dunno."

"What time did you get there that night?"

"I dunno. I just remember shooting, that's all."

"You have no memory prior to . . . that?"

"No, man. How many times I gotta say it. No. I remember shooting her, and coming into the group session, and telling them about it. But I don't remember nothing before. Nothing."

"William, if you didn't do it—"

"What the fuck is wrong with you, Jack? Watch my fucking lips. I shot her. I . . . shot . . . her. Got it? No question."

"Bear with me, huh? Please?"

"Not if you keep talking shit."

"I need your help on this, William. If you didn't do it, then whoever did was smart enough to set you up gift-wrapped. My guess is neither McCatty nor Bjorkman is that smart. Or sly. Is there anybody you think—"

"Man, that's it! That's fucking it! What do you think—you can look inside my head and tell me that something that's there isn't?" He pointed to his temple. "There's a memory in here, Jack. A picture of me pulling the trigger on her, that fucking little two-timing bitch. I killed her, I fucking killed her. Why you making me go over it again and again, man? You wanna drive me crazy?''

''William, you said that the hypnosis did you some good at the beginning, but then—''

William was already standing. ''Get laid, motherfucker.''

He motioned to the guard and left.

EIGHTEEN

As I drove south toward Marion, I tried to sort out what
little I had learned from William. Racial taunts from all
sides, difficulty in adjusting to life on academia's fast
track—these were things I'd expected, given my talks with
others. What was harder to figure was his jumping from
street slang to classroom eloquence, from vague cooperation to flaring hostility, every time I mentioned Jennifer,
sex, or both together. I decided to check in with Dr. Lopez
at U Mass if time permitted.

I swung onto Route 24, taking it south to where Route
25 branches off to the left. Slowing and winding for intermittent construction, I got onto Interstate 195 for a few
miles to the Marion exit. I eased up on the gas pedal,
glancing frequently at Mrs. Wald's intricate but apparently
accurate directions. I also began to get a feel for the town.

Marion is located on a cove off Buzzards Bay. While

not a joy to the ear, Buzzards Bay is moneyland, the south-western terminus of the Cape Cod Canal, the ambitious construction project that transformed the Cape from a peninsula into an island. The canal permitted boat passage from Cape Cod Bay southwest toward the fingery southern coast of Rhode Island, thereby bringing high real estate prices and prosperity to the towns located on Buzzards Bay. In Marion, however, both prices and prosperity had been high for generations, the town being one of the summer enclaves for the old rich and the very rich (with the fabulously rich going to Newport, Rhode Island, and the nouveau rich slumming it on the Cape).

As I ran out of turns to make, the olde family compounds (two or three understated houses sharing tennis courts and wide lawns to the cove) began to get smaller and more compacted. Soon I was in a more commercial district and then, on my last left fork, I came into a neighborhood of amateurish summer homes converted to year-round use. I slowed and stopped in front of a parked moving van with its wide ramp already down.

I got out and walked toward the door of the house. A tall, slim girl in her late teens was talking to a boxcar of a man in blue work pants and a strappie undershirt.

The man said, "And, honey, I'm tellin' ya, the kid and I can take it out, but we gotta take the door off the hinges."

She said, "The guy on the phone didn't say anything about that."

The man was sounding exasperated. "Look, the guy on the phone, he didn't see the door, for chrissakes. He's calling from Falmouth and buying a baby grand from Marion and he probably doesn't know you ain't got double French doors opening into the garden, y'know?" The man looked inside and barked, "Jimmy, for chrissakes, leave that till I tell ya, huh?"

"I don't remember them having to take the door off to get it in," said the girl, stubbornly.

"Then they musta built the house around it." He called inside again. "Jimmy, come out here." The man turned to the girl. "Tell ya what. Me and Jimmy are gonna take a break, walk back to that coffee shop down to the main road. You think about it, call your mother, whatever you want. We'll be back in half an hour. Then either the door comes off or we take off."

A freckled kid edged sideways past the girl, who was holding her ground in the doorway. He was maybe sixteen and stared at her rump as he moved by her.

As the man passed me, he muttered, "Fucking college. Doesn't have the brains God gave . . ."

I missed the next part as Jimmy said, "Fuckin' A, Uncle Vin," and followed the big man down the path.

The girl looked at me for the first time. "You're too late. We already sold the piano."

I gestured toward the departing pair. "Maybe not."

She sighed, looked at the door. "What if they can't get it back on?"

"If they can get it off, they can get it back on. So long as they don't break or bend anything."

She turned back to me, cocked her head. "You aren't here for the piano, are you?"

"No, my name is John Cuddy. I'm—"

"You're the one who called last night. About Jennifer."

"That's right. Your mother—"

"Can I see some identification, please?"

Smart kid. I showed her. She examined it, then said, "Mom said you were from the police. That's not what that says."

"I told your mother I was a detective investigating Jennifer's death. She may have assumed—"

"What you wanted her to assume." Deborah gave me a scrunched-up smile. "Come in anyway."

As she walked in front of me into the house, I could see why Jimmy was admiring her. She had on faded cut-off jean short-shorts and beautiful legs marred only by matching varicose veins on the backs of her calves. I could also see why Uncle Vin was ticked at her. The baby grand occupied at least half of the old cottage's living room.

She pointed me toward a stuffed armchair and seated herself in its mate across from me. "So how come you're still investigating when they have William already?"

"I'm working with William's lawyer. There are a lot of disparities in what happened. I'm hoping you'll be able to tell me something that will help."

"Help William get off, you mean."

"Help find who's really responsible."

"Don't expect any miracles."

"I won't."

"Okay. What do you want to know?"

"I understand that William met Jennifer at Goreham, in the dorms."

"That's right. Her boyfriend of the hour was hassling him or something and she picked him up. At least, to hear her tell it."

"By 'boyfriend of the hour' I take it you mean she was pretty popular?"

Deborah stifled a laugh. "Yeah, she was 'popular.' Or maybe I ought to say 'copular,' if that's a word. Because that was what she did best."

"I thought you two were roommates."

"We were."

"Doesn't sound like you were too close."

She shifted in the chair, feigning relaxation. "We didn't get along too well."

"How do you mean?"

She shifted again. "Look, I don't see how this can possibly matter to you. About William, I mean."

"I need to find out everything I can about Jennifer. I didn't know her, and if someone other than William killed her, then I . . ."

"All right. My dad died of cancer. Three months ago, all right? I found out—he found out he had it just before Thanksgiving. And Jennifer was a shit about it, an absolute shit. I mean, I'd be in my room, crying, for God's sake, and she'd be sticking her head around the door, trying to get me to leave for a while because she had some guy with her. She wouldn't go out to dinner with me, or talk with me, or even just listen to me. Understand?"

"I understand."

"No, you don't." She started to get teary. "You couldn't understand unless you were losing someone to cancer a day at a time like I was. Someone you loved."

"Like I said."

She was about to cry, then bit it off, assessing me. "One of your parents?"

"My wife."

"God," she said. "But you're so . . . I . . . I'm sorry, I didn't mean . . ."

"That's okay. It was a while ago. I can talk about it now. It gets a little easier as time goes on."

Her face reset a bit, the tears on hold. "That's funny. Odd, I mean. I wanted to talk about it. With him, with my mother, but they're . . . My father survived the camps. In Germany, the death camps. He was just a baby, but he got out and came to this country when he was seven. He went to pharmacy school, and he opened his own drugstore here. I was thirteen, thirteen, before I ever found out about him in the camps, and them from some man who

141

called here one day, looking for money for a Holocaust observance. My father never talked about it. But I got interested in Judaism, like in my roots, you know, and Goreham's got a great religion department, and then David was going there already.''

"David?"

She darkened. "Just a guy I knew from here. There aren't many Jews in this town. I dated him in high school. He's a junior at Goreham now."

I thought back to my visit to McCatty and something Mrs. Creasey had started to say. "Exams all over?"

"I'm sorry. What?"

"Exams. At school. I thought exams were still in progress there, but your mother said you were working around here."

"I, uh, had to leave school. Between my dad and . . . all."

"And all?"

"Look, I don't mean to be rude, but this is my personal life and I still don't see what it has to do with William."

"If 'and all' doesn't involve Jennifer, we can skip it."

She crossed her arms, waggled her foot at me. "Jennifer and I double-dated, her with a kind of creepy guy named Dick McCatty and me with David. This was maybe two weeks before . . . before we found out about my dad."

"I've met McCatty."

"Anyway, I thought it went okay. Jennifer seemed to get along with David, and I was glad. I mean, she was my roommate, and he was my boyfriend, and, you know, I was glad they liked each other. Well, I got the news about my dad, and I needed someone to talk to. Bad. But Jennifer wasn't in our room, and the only other girl in the dorm that I knew well enough was in class somewhere, so I ran over to David's place—he has an apartment just off campus. I get there and run up the stairs and I'm starting to cry, I mean the news about my dad was just starting to sink in, so I pounded on his door, and nobody came, so I kept pounding and pounding. Finally I hear him inside, cursing but coming, and he opens the door just a little bit, and I kind of push past him. That's when I see he's got just a towel on, and the door to his bedroom is open, and there's Jennifer stretched out on his bed, and . . . Well, I just ran out of there. He tried to grab me and was saying something to me, but I broke away from him and got out of there and just ran and cried and . . ."

Deborah began crying, deeply and regularly, as though she were still running and crying that day and needed to breathe correctly to be able to do both at once. I saw a Kleenex box on an end table near the couch and brought it over to her. She stabbed at it, bringing a wad to her eyes and nose. In about a minute, she stopped, snuffled a few times, and bunched the used tissues in her fist.

"I'm sorry," I said.

"It's okay . . . It's just that even after that, I mean, they didn't know about my dad, and I didn't have any leash on David, but when I waited for Jennifer to say something to me, explain at least, if not apologize, she never did. She acted toward me like I wasn't there. No, that's not right. She acted as though I was there, but that nothing had happened. She'd come back to the room and try to make small talk about class or clothes or whatever, like my dad wasn't dying and like I hadn't caught . . . yes, caught her with David." She sniffed again, but appeared over the worst part.

"Did Jennifer ever talk much about William?"

"Oh, yeah. Till I had to make her shut up. She went on about how great he was in bed, how exciting it was to . . . well, do things with a black guy. Then . . ."

"Then?"

"Then, I don't know exactly, but she started saying things like sometimes he . . . he was like impotent, you know? Of course, he was under a lot of pressure."

"At school, you mean?"

"Oh, yeah, that too, for sure. I mean, he struck me as pretty bright and all, but you could tell just listening to him talk that he hadn't had a really good early education. But I meant mainly from Jennifer. She used to show him off, on her arm like some rare bird, the inner-city tamed stud, you know?"

"Would you guess Jennifer was involved with other boys while she was seeing William? Besides David, I mean."

"No guessing about it." Deborah shook her ponytail and leaned forward earnestly. "Look, I know I'm being pretty rough on her and all, but she really was an incredible little bitch. She wanted to sample it all, and with her looks and money, she really could."

"She ever talk about the psychotherapy group she was in?"

"Yeah." Deborah looked down at the clump of tissues in her hand. "I'm going to throw these away. Can I get you something to drink?"

"Just some water would be great."

"Be right back."

She left the room. I decided David was a jerk. An understandable jerk, maybe, but a jerk nonetheless.

She returned and handed me a tall glass, brimming with little ice cubes.

"Thank you."

Deborah said, "Actually, Jennifer didn't say too much about that—the psychotherapy stuff, I mean. I had the impression that she didn't think too much of the people in it, except for the shrink himself."

"Clifford Marek?"

"Yeah, that was the name. She had the hots for him too, surprise, surprise."

"Do you think they were involved?"

"Funny . . . no, I don't. I mean, Jennifer talked about him a lot at first, and I think she got William to start going partly to sort of please Marek—he was trying to get some kind of real mixed group together, for research or something, I guess. I think Marek kind of kept his distance from her, like either he was too ethical to go after a patient or he could tell she might be trouble. Besides, I was just the one Jennifer bragged to. She confided in someone else."

"Who?"

"This woman in her group. She has an odd first name, like some singer my mother used to like."

"Lainie?"

"That's right. Lainie. I remember Jennifer saying she thought Lainie really had the world all figured out."

Three loud knocks came at the front door. Deborah said, "Oh, shit, they're back." She looked at me. "Do you think I should let them take the door off?"

"It depends. They probably can't get the piano out any other way."

"You said it depends?"

"On how badly you want the piano out of here."

They knocked again. Deborah yelled, "I'm coming." She turned back to me. "Oh, I want it out, all right. My father used to play it. Every night before bed. I guess in the camp there was an orchestra—remember the big fight over whether Vanessa Redgrave should be in that TV movie?"

"I remember."

"Well, my father said the reason he wouldn't talk about

the camp was that there was only one good thing he associated with it, and that was the music. So every night he played here. Kind of a testament, I guess."

"But you want the piano out?"

"Yeah," she said, getting up. I stood too. She continued, "My mother can't look at it without crying, and in this room, it's kind of hard to miss."

They knocked again. "Okay, okay," she called.

I said to her, "Thank you for all your time."

"That's all right." She dropped to the softer voice again. "Can I ask you a question?"

"Sure."

"Before, when you told me about your wife, you weren't just using that to get me to talk to you, were you?"

"I hope not."

She smiled a little and we moved to the door. Uncle Vin was there, Jimmy in his shadow.

"Well?" said Uncle Vin.

"You can take the door off," said Deborah.

"Thank God," said Uncle Vin as they went in and I went out.

"Fuckin' A," whispered Jimmy.

NINETEEN

♦

As I drove away from the Walds' neighborhood, I spotted the coffee shop that Uncle Vin had mentioned. Next to it was a pay phone in one of those vertical glass coffins. I pulled in alongside.

Fortunately, it was push-button, so using my credit card was relatively easy. First I called my answering service. There were two messages, one from Lieutenant Murphy and one from Mrs. Daniels, both essentially seeking status reports. I tried Murphy first and spoke with a young homicide detective named Cross, whom I'd met with Murphy. She said the lieutenant was out, but she'd give him my message.

I called directory assistance for Lainie Bishop's number. She had two listed, one business and one home. I dialed the business number and after four rings got a harried answering service who took down my information and assured me that Ms. Bishop would return my call. I tried Lainie's home phone and after two rings got Lainie's voice on telephone tape. After dutifully waiting for the beep, I left a message saying I wanted to see her that night, at her house if preferable to her.

Next was Mariah Lopez. I'd interrupted a session she was having with a student, but she said she would be available at 4:30 P.M. for half an hour if I could come to U Mass then. I checked my watch and told her I'd be there.

Last, I reached Mrs. Daniels at work. I told her I'd like to see her that night. She suggested seven-thirty, and I said fine.

For the ride back to Boston, I swung east and took Route 3A, the so-called shore route, north. Route 3A used to be slower but a lot more scenic than Route 3, the extension of the Southeast Expressway. Route 3A is still slower, but the scenery has been replaced by the kind of strip-city fast-foods and mini-malls you see in the Midwest.

I arrived at U Mass about four-fifteen, and got in to see Dr. Lopez at four-thirty on the nose.

"Well," she said, "have you found out anything that helps William?"

"A little, but also some that hurts him."

"What can I do?"

"I'm not sure. I'd like to bounce some of my impressions off you and see what you think."

"All right."

"It seems that William's relationship with the dead girl was not exactly a storybook romance."

"They seldom are these days."

"I don't want to be crude, but—"

"Mr. Cuddy, I really have heard most everything in this job that could possibly shock me, and I haven't run for the convent yet."

I laughed politely and said, "I confirmed that Jennifer was sleeping around. A lot. It also seems that William would have had to be deaf and blind not to realize it."

"I already told you that would hurt William."

"Maybe not. I've been wondering why William picked the time and place it appears he did to kill her. I mean, they were together in a lot more available places than the boiler room of their psychiatrist's office building. Also, if his motive was that she was cheating on him, he knew about that long ago."

"And therefore?"

"If it's a crime of passion, it should have happened sooner. If it's premeditated, why not pick a better spot?"

She looked thoughtful. "You recall that I haven't seen William for quite some time?"

"Yes."

"Well, if he was under the kinds of pressures that I believe he was, then it is possible that those pressures would have taken some time to reach an intolerable level."

"Granted, but when I spoke with William at the jail, he was rational and helpful with most of the topics we covered. Where he blew his top was over Jennifer and the night she died."

"Given the circumstances of her death, that's rather understandable, isn't it?"

"He vented in a sexual way, a cursing way. He was like a student speaking in a classroom discussion, until I would mention Jennifer, then it was 'that bitch' and 'that slut' and so on. He even tried to insult my sexuality."

A smile started at the corner of her mouth, but she clamped it down. "William is a poor black male who was involved with a wealthy white girl who, as you say, slept around. Mostly with white males?"

"I'm not sure, but I would think so."

"Well, then, he probably views you as a potential, and likely successful, competitor for Jennifer. Even though she's dead, he would still see you through that sort of lens."

As he might view Marek, if William saw Jennifer playing up to him. Which could explain the timing and the site of her death, but not in a way that would help my client.

"Mr. Cuddy?"

"Sorry; lost in thought."

"Is there anything more I can help you with?"

"There are a few more people I need to see. Did you come up with anyone that I could talk to about drugs and hypnosis?"

"One possibility, but I want to speak with him first myself. So that he knows you'll be contacting him."

"I understand. If you can, please just call and leave me a message."

"Certainly."

She let me use her phone to call my answering service. No return word from Lainie.

When I got back down to my car, there was a campus police parking ticket on it. I glanced at my watch. Only four-fifty. I'd told Mrs. Daniels seven-thirty. The crosstown traffic would be murder now, so there was no sense trying to check my mail at the office or the condo. I smiled. Plenty of time for a dinner at Amrhein's and a visit.

"I had the pot roast, kid. Mashed potatoes, gravy, fresh green beans."

Heineken?

"Yes, but just two with dinner."

And how many with dessert?

"Very funny." I bent down, smoothed the white, whispery wrapping around the mums. "Mrs. Feeney went back to the good paper. She said one complaint from as old and loyal a customer as me was enough."

Did she emphasize the "loyal" or the "old"?

"I'm glad one of us has a sense of humor tonight."

Nancy?

"No. I mean, no, I haven't heard from her yet." She lived just about five blocks from where I was standing. "It's about this case."

The black student and his girlfriend?

"Yes. Some things still seem awfully convenient, but you have those in any investigation because you have them happening in real life, the real life that the investigation looks back at. Given that William confessed and was there and had the gun, the police didn't feel they had to look into many corners. And to be fair to the cops, most of the things I've found hurt William as much as help him."

So what are you going to do now?

"Play out the string. Talk to a few more people, check back on a couple I've already seen."

Have you changed your mind about whether he did it?

I didn't answer. In the harbor below us, the sailboats were tacking and turning about in that odd, Grecian urn style of almost-tag they play. I felt the same way, reaching out for something I couldn't seem to touch.

John?

"I still can't prove he didn't kill her."

Have you thought about it from the other viewpoint?

"If he didn't do it, somebody else must have?"

Yes.

"Yeah, I've thought about it. But the ones with motives, and arguably the knowledge of hypnosis, like McCatty or Bjorkman, don't have the sophistication to bring it off. And the ones with the knowledge and the nerve to do it, like Marek and maybe Homer Linden, don't have the motive.''

That you know of.

''You're right. I'll keep digging.'' I turned toward the car, then back. ''Oh, by the way. The dead girl, Jennifer . . .''

I haven't seen her here.

''I'm not surprised.''

I pulled onto Millrose Street and found a spot four doors from Mrs. Daniels's house. As I got out of the car, I thought I saw Stooper, the second black kid from my previous visit, scurry off some steps and into an alley between two burned-out shells. Probably not struck with fright at the sight of me.

Mrs. Daniels answered the door so quickly I thought she must have been standing next to it waiting for me. She offered me tea again, but I declined. We sat in the same places in the living room that we had last time.

''Was William more helpful to you today?''

''Yes, much.'' A little embroidering might make her feel better. ''Mrs. Daniels, the reason I wanted to see you was to tell you that I still don't have proof that William didn't kill Jennifer Creasey, but that, for what it's worth, I don't believe he did.''

Tears welled up in her eyes. She used the edge of her right index finger to wipe them away. ''You don't know . . .'' She caught herself, then continued. ''You don't know how good that is to hear. You're the first . . . oh, his lawyer, Mr. Rothenberg, has been very kind, and I know he's trying for William, but I just have the feeling he doesn't really believe that William's innocent.''

''Mrs. Daniels, if William didn't do it, then somebody went to an awful lot of trouble to make it seem that he did. Is there anyone you know of that might hate William enough to do that?''

"No. I mean, not that I ever met. But the girl was keeping company with another boy at the college before William.''

"Richard McCatty. For a lot of reasons, I doubt it would be him.''

She paused. "There's really no one else I can think of. I mean, the street kids here, they'd never go out there to pull something." Her face became concerned. "They didn't bother you tonight, did they?''

"No, they didn't. Mrs. Daniels, I've very nearly run out of people to talk to. Would it be all right with you if I looked through William's room?''

"You mean, like through his papers and things?''

"Yes.''

"The police already did that, you know. With a warrant and all, weeks ago.''

"Did you see what they took?''

"Yes, just a couple of pictures of William with the girl and a couple of the girl herself. They even made me sign for them, like a receipt. Didn't send me a copy of the receipt like they said they would. Does that make a difference?''

"Probably not. I'd still like to see his things, though.''

"Sure. If they couldn't hurt him, maybe they can help him.''

She led me up a hardwood staircase that was carefully polished. The steps could have used refinishing, however, and the worn narrow gray runner replacing. We turned right at the top of the stairs, and she opened a closed door. "This is William's. Do you want me to stay or do you want to be alone?''

"Stay, please.''

She sat on a rickety wooden desk chair, partially pulled out from a cheap metal desk with an old, battered Royal portable on it. Next to the desk were a bureau and a closet. A single twin bed lay flush against a second wall and under a window that showed the small yard behind the house. Some bookshelves leaned precariously against the third wall, less a function of poor construction than of chronic overcrowding.

"William has a lot of books."

"Oh, yes, he read . . . reads a lot. The jail, they let me bring him books, but he doesn't seem to want them."

The shelves contained almost all paperbacks, many looking as if he'd bought them used. Some best-sellers, mysteries, and science fiction, but overwhelmingly college course books, poetry, psychology, history, political science, and so on. A remarkably comprehensive personal library.

I crossed to the desk. Mrs. Daniels moved over to the bed. I went through the papers on his desk, which seemed to be typed rough drafts of schoolwork. I opened each of the three drawers in succession. Old Corrasable bond, pencils, erasers, baseball cards, coins, newspaper clippings, report cards, class pictures, and the various other crap that student desks have always accumulated.

"Mrs. Daniels, did William have any secret hiding place, somewhere he might have put things he wouldn't want anyone else to see?"

She looked around the room, shook her head. "If he did, he kept it from me."

Framed on the bureau was a five-by-seven photograph of a younger William standing with Mrs. Daniels next to him. William wore a cap and gown, clutching a diploma in his upraised fist. Both mother and son sported broad smiles.

"High school graduation," she said. "Seems a long time ago."

I pushed the desk out from the wall. Nothing taped to it. I took out all the drawers. Nothing. Under the desk frame. Same. The bureau and the bed. Same. Through the closet, past shoes, a baseball glove, a deflated plastic football, and assorted clothing. Same. Under a pile of three cheap sweaters on the top shelf, however, I found a small tape player, designed like a blaster but fancier, with a built-in mike and what looked like a voice-activated recorder button. I pulled it down and examined it. There was a tape still in it.

"The girl gave that to William. For Christmas. He was ashamed because all he could give her was some kind of little perfume bottle that he still had to go without lunch three weeks to buy."

I ejected the tape. Its label was marked DEMONSTRATION TAPE, NOT FOR RESALE. On each side was printed an awkward title in English, with a Japanese performer's name in parentheses after it.

"William have many tapes?"

"No. I mean, I never saw him use that thing. I think it reminded him that he couldn't afford to give her anything so nice."

I popped the tape back in and pressed the Play button. After some whirring static, lute and mandolin music began. As I was about to hit the Stop button, William's voice, very hushed, came on.

"Thursday, March eleventh, eleven-thirty P.M." That was six weeks before Jennifer was killed. There was a change in the background noise after he said "P.M." I turned the volume up and up without effect until a sound blared from the speakers and bounced off the walls like a wild animal that wanted out. As I turned it down, Mrs.

Daniels yelled, "Oh, God, oh, God, turn it off, turn it off!"

The noise had sounded like a young man screaming.

Mrs. Daniels was crying hoarsely. "That's William . . . that's William. From his nightmares . . . Oh, God, he taped them, so he could hear . . . himself. . . . Oh, God."

I let her go for a minute or two, getting some Kleenex from the bathroom for her. I took the desk chair, she stayed on the bed. She slowed down, dried her tears, looked up red-eyed. "I'm sorry," she said.

"That's all right. Can you talk about it now?"

"Yes," she said, swiping at her nose with the tissues. "I'm fine now."

"William was having nightmares?"

"Yes."

"When?"

"About the time he started going to Goreham. No." She sniffled. "No, more like Thanksgiving time. He wasn't doing well there, his grades and all the other stuff must have been weighing on him more than I knew. Then he moved home here, and he started having these terrible nightmares. Not often, but he'd cry out, in the middle of the night, so . . . so piteous, like a wounded creature. He would cry out and I'd come running into his room. I mean, he was in college, but he was still my son, and he'd be all tensed up and sweating, like on his stomach, but with his head on the pillow and halfway up on his knees, like a little child hiding from the dark. And I'd try to hold him, but he'd fight me off, even"—she lowered and slowed her voice—"even hit me once, and he never hit me, not ever, but he was still asleep and he didn't know what he was doing, didn't know it was me, even. But then he'd finally wake up and he'd be crying and shivering like he was freezing to death, even with the heat on and all. It was awful when they came, the nightmares. Just awful."

"Did he ever see anybody about them?"

"I told William to talk to that psychiatrist he was seeing. Or at least Dr. Lopez over to U Mass, but he never would tell me whether he did."

"Can I take the machine and tape with me?"

"Well, yes, I guess. Do you think they can help him?"

"They may help me."

"Then take them, please."

She promised me she would look to see if there were any more tapes lying around. I made what I hoped were reassuring noises while she showed me out the door.

As I walked down her steps and turned toward my car, I was looking at the tape machine instead of ahead of me. Stupid.

I was less than twenty feet from them before an odd sound made me look up properly. My three friends from last time were lounging on the same stoop, smiling at me in a superior way. Leaning against my car, his rump on the driver's-side window ledge, was another, older black, maybe six-one and carrying a muscular two forty or so inside his sleeveless sweatshirt. He was swinging a tire chain casually with his left hand against my door. He must have just started with the chain, because it was making the noise that caused me to look up, a drumming like intermittent hail on a tin roof.

"Welcome back," said the kid I remembered as Negotiator.

"Nice to see you adapting to the culture," said Stooper, bobbing his head toward the tape machine.

I shifted the thing to my left hand, holding it by the handle across my stomach. "How's the protection business?" I asked.

"Little slow," said Negotiator, "till you come along."

"What makes you think it's going to pick up?"

Stooper gestured magnanimously and spoke in a falsetto voice. "Perhaps you haven't met my dear brother, Floyd." Stooper lowered his tone back to normal. "Floyd, he like two things. Movies and the money to see 'em with."

Negotiator said, "He hate two things too. You and your car."

I looked over at big Floyd. He smiled and accentuated the arc and therefore the sound of his weapon.

"The tire chain for me or the car?"

"The car," said Negotiator.

"You," said Stooper.

"Maybe both," said Third.

Floyd grinned malevolently. I said to him, "You must be a real prodigy, Floyd. Hired muscle for three punk kids. What's the matter, the barbells cut off the blood to your brain?"

Floyd stopped smiling. He came off the car and began swinging the tire chain like a samurai. Around, across, over, intersecting but varying patterns. Unfortunately, he looked like he knew what he was doing. He took two steps toward me and repeated the show.

"So, Floyd, you like movies, right?" I said, slipping my right hand behind the tape player and toward the left front of my belt. "You remember *Raiders of the Lost Ark?* The market scene?"

"Say what?" said Floyd, coming two steps closer.

I drew my gun and leveled it at his chest. His face dropped a few inches and he ran his tongue over his lips. He backed up and I started forward. We kept moving that way, he maintaining the same distance as we approached my car.

Stooper recovered first. "He ain't got the balls to shoot, Floyd."

"That's not the issue, fellas," I said, setting down the tape player, but keeping my eyes and gun on the now stationary Floyd. I put the key in the lock and opened the door. "The issue is whether Floyd has the balls to find out."

Negotiator chimed in. "He bullshitting you, Floyd. He shoot you, he lose his license. He won't shoot. It ain't like the movies."

"You're right there, my friend," I said, gently tossing the tape machine onto the passenger seat. I rolled down the driver's-side window and got in. "It's not like the movies. Out here, dead is forever."

I started up and pulled out fast, ducking a little, then checking the mirror. Nobody had moved by the time I was half a block away.

TWENTY

I parked the car behind the building and carried William's music box up to the condo. I called my answering service and checked my telephone tape machine. Still nothing from Lainie.

I set the blaster on the coffee table and mixed myself a strong screwdriver. I drank half of it, changing to a pair of tennis shorts and a sweater. Then I rewound the tape to the beginning and, being careful to modulate the volume, listened to the tape in its entirety.

It was, in effect, an oral diary of William's nightmares. Each entry started with William's whispered statement of day, date, and time. Then dead airspace, then nerve-curdling screams as the voice-activated trigger kicked the machine on during the night. There were five entries altogether, on three of which I could hear Mrs. Daniels's frightened but soothing talking after two minutes or so of horror. Not much of William's screaming involved discernible words. I clearly heard a few "No, no" passages and twice I thought I heard him say, "Please, no more, it hurts, it hurts," or something close to it. Aside from the screaming, the only consistent theme was that each entry was on either a Thursday or a Friday.

I rewound and replayed several times the passages where I thought words were being spoken. I stopped after that. It was pretty gruesome stuff, and I knew that there were enhancement techniques that could bring out more detail if it proved important later on.

I finished a second screwdriver and thought seriously about a third. I was still on an adrenaline high from the incident with the street kids, and I weighed the dulling effect of the drink against the increased chance it would give me my own nightmares. I decided I was being silly and had the drink. And the nightmares.

The hammering at my door woke me up the next morning. Having dropped off on the couch, I was still dressed. I moved to the door, trying to remember if I had heard the downstairs, building door buzzer. I was pretty sure I hadn't.

"Who is it?" I asked through the wood.

"Detective Cross. Open up."

I recognized her voice and unlocked the door.

Her eyes looked bloodshot. So did those of Paul O'Boy, standing behind her.

"Can we come in?" she said.

"Sure."

I led them into the living room and pointed toward the sofa. The music box was still on the coffee table, but there wasn't much I could do about that now. They both sat down, looking about as comfortable as a priest and a nun on a blind date.

"I don't drink it myself, but there's probably some instant coffee around somewhere if you'd like."

They both said "No" quickly. Odd. Cops after long nights always want coffee.

I took a leather chair across from them. "So how do I merit this interjurisdictional visit?"

"Detective O'Boy?" said Cross, staring down at her knees.

O'Boy looked up at me. "I'd like you to come with me. The chief wants to talk with you."

"Your chief?"

"Naturally my chief."

"What about?"

O'Boy chewed on his lip. "He said not to tell you."

Cross kept looking at her knees. I sank back in my chair. "What the hell is going on here?" I said.

"Chief Wooten has some questions he wants to ask you," said Cross.

"I gathered that. Questions about what?"

"Jesus, Cuddy," she said, looking up. "Can't you just go with the guy?"

"Why? Because he's asking politely?"

"Why not?"

I leaned forward. "I'll tell you why not. First, it's barely dawn. Second, O'Boy here doesn't just call me and say, 'Could you stop out here sometime today?' He drives twenty miles to arrive unannounced at my doorstep with a beat Boston homicide cop as shotgun guard. That suggests to me a big-time problem with a short-term deadline for O'Boy's chief. That makes me want to hear a reason why I should go with him."

O'Boy worked his hands as if he was lathering them with soap. "Cuddy, you were in the service, right?"

"Yeah."

"MPs," said Cross.

O'Boy said, "Then you can understand the spot I'm in. The chief says bring you in, but not to tell you why. What can I do?"

"Sure you won't have some coffee?" I said, settling back into the chair as though I had all day.

Cross read the hint. "Cuddy, with what he's got, he might be able to get a warrant."

"Arrest or search?"

She said, "Look, why force something that might embarrass someone?"

Meaning Murphy? I watched her closely. She was tired and on the verge of decking me, but she was trying to pull off a distasteful task professionally.

"I'll go with him," I said. "He can drive his car, and I can drive mine."

O'Boy said, "Cuddy . . ."

I said, "Or I can drive his car and he can drive mine."

O'Boy moved his head, more in resignation than in disagreement. "I'll follow you out there."

I got up and moved to the coffee table. "This thing's busted," I said, picking up the blaster, "but I can turn on the stereo if you'd like some music while I shower and shave."

Cross looked up at me as though she wished she carried a concealed chainsaw. I took William's machine into the bedroom and got ready as quickly as I could.

O'Boy drove Cross to her apartment house in the South End, then followed me as I wound him out of there and to the Mass Pike. We made it to Calem in about thirty-five minutes. Parking in the police lot, we walked abreast into the station house.

O'Boy put me in the same room I'd seen before. He returned ten minutes later with a slim, crew-cut man in a turquoise short-sleeved sport shirt. There was a fading Navy tattoo on the man's right forearm and an unlit filterless cigarette in the man's mouth.

O'Boy said, "Chief Wooten, John Cuddy."

"Chief," I said.

Wooten turned to O'Boy. "He been frisked and advised of his right?"

O'Boy reddened. "No, Chief."

"Do it."

I felt sorry for O'Boy, so I assumed the position against the wall while O'Boy gave me a desultory pat-down and recited this year's interpretation of *Miranda* and *Escobedo*. I sat back down.

"Where were you last night from four P.M. onward?" said Wooten.

"I want a lawyer," I said.

Wooten turned angrily to O'Boy. "You said he'd cooperate."

"I would have," I said.

"What do you mean?" said Wooten.

"Just what I said. I would have."

"Then why aren't you?" said Wooten.

"Because I don't like the sudden onset of Bjorkman syndrome I see in you, Chief. Tell me, does old Georgie remind you of yourself when you were young?"

O'Boy didn't know where to look, so he just squeezed his eyes shut. What little flesh there was on Wooten's face stretched back taut. "Who the hell do you think you are, mister?"

"A private investigator who twice has come, without any trouble, to your station. I'm guessing you've got a major coronary coming on, since last time you wanted me gone forever and this time you want me back before breakfast. Now, if you stop playing Felony Squad with me, I'll be happy to cooperate. Okay?''

"Chief," said O'Boy, "can we be straight with him?"

Wooten just glared at me.

"Chief?" said O'Boy again.

Wooten spoke with difficulty. "Lainie Bishop was found dead last night, Cuddy. Your voice was on her telephone machine, saying you were going to meet her. Now account for your whereabouts. Without any shit on the edges."

I went through my timetable from 4:00 P.M. onward: Mariah Lopez's office, dinner at Amrhein's, Mrs. Feeney's shop, Beth's grave, Mrs. Daniels's house. I skipped the street kids and William's tape player.

"You figure that covers you until about nine P.M.," said Wooten.

"More like nine-thirty, I'd say."

"Word of a charged murderer's mother isn't exactly gospel."

I added the street kids, explaining how they could verify my arrival and departure, but still deleting the music box. "When was she killed?"

Wooten looked disgusted and took a chair. O'Boy said, "Medical examiner'll try to pin it down closer, but we got a real estate customer putting her alive at four-thirty P.M. and a date finding the back door busted and her dead at eight-thirty P.M."

"Her house?"

"Yeah."

"B and E?"

Wooten said, "Looks like it now."

"Chief," I said, "just because I have an alibi doesn't automatically make it a panicked burglar."

Wooten flared up again. "Her skull was broke open by a poker from her fireplace, and the sliding glass door to a back deck was jimmied. We got the Daniels kid in the slam, no motive for the date who shows up, and four houses hit similar in town in the last three months. What does it add up to to you?''

"Any violence in the other hits?''

"No,'' said Wooten.

"Same time of day?''

"No.''

"M.O. of the other hits in the paper?''

O'Boy said, "Local weekly's called the *Chronicle*. It runs a 'Police Blotter' column. Editor says they were all in it, with enough details to warn the home owners.''

"Or to tutor a guy who's copycatting or masking.''

"Masking what?'' said Wooten.

"If somebody other than Daniels killed the Creasey girl, then maybe the somebody killed Lainie Bishop and masked it to look like a burglary.''

Wooten looked exasperated. "Cuddy, do you know how many witnesses there were to Daniels's confession? He had the gun, the motive, the opportunity, blood on his shirt. God almighty. The Daniels boy did the first, and some other junkie from Rox' did this one.''

"C'mon, Chief. You didn't buy that before you heard my alibi, and you shouldn't buy it now. Two women from the same five-patient therapy group are murdered in your town inside a month and they're not connected? How many other homicides you had in this town in the last ten years? Three?''

O'Boy said, "Two other than these here.''

Wooten stood up. "Cuddy, I've about had my fill of you. Come up with some hard evidence, and I'll be all ears. Till then, why'n't you peddle your theories someplace else?'' He looked to O'Boy. "Drive him back when and if you get the time.''

O'Boy and I stayed silent until Wooten closed the door behind him.

I said, "Commander like that makes the days seem longer."

O'Boy started to say something, stopped, and said, "The chief's a good cop. You give him something to sink his teeth into, he's like a bulldog."

"Come on, O'Boy. Doesn't this case stink to you too?"

"I dunno."

"Jesus."

"Awright. Say, just for the sake of argument, now, that some guy other than Daniels really kills the Creasey girl. When Daniels confesses, the guy's home free. Why spoil it by killing Lainie Bishop?"

"Blackmail?"

"By Bishop, you mean?"

"Yeah."

"Okay. So he pays her. For a while, to let things cool down. Then kills her. Maybe somewheres else. Like on a vacation. Broad like her, she musta liked Club Med or whatever. Wait it out."

"Maybe she wants the earth and the moon."

"So he goes in hock for a while to pay her. Good investment if you need the time and your neck's on the line."

"O'Boy, you in touch with anybody else from the therapy group about the Bishop killing?"

"No. Well . . . the old guy. Linden?"

"Homer Linden."

"Yeah, the guy that looks like a corpse. When I pulled up to Bishop's house, Linden was already there, talking to one of the uniforms. Claimed he heard the dispatcher on his police scanner radio."

"Pretty convenient."

"The guy only lives around the corner."

167

"A little farther. I've been there. Who was the date?"

"Huh?"

"Bishop's date. The one who found her."

"Oh, some computer troubleshooter. He's here for two days, staying at the Marriott in Newton. He meets her in some bar coupla months ago, dukes her that night, and calls to set up a 'date' for last night. Guy's married, from Rochester, for chrissakes. I give him a lot of credit for even calling it in to us."

"Who was the uniform?"

"That talked to Linden?"

"Yeah."

"Clay. You met him."

"I thought he and Bjorkman were on the day shift?"

"They were. Rotated onto four to twelve yesterday."

O'Boy wouldn't give me Clay's home number or address but said he'd leave word for Clay to call me when he came in for his tour. I thanked him and slipped out of the building and lot without Wooten seeing I was under my own power.

I had a little trouble finding Homer's house again, but got the right street on the third try. I rang his bell.

After two minutes the door opened. He did a double take, then smiled. "Come in, come in."

TWENTY-ONE

"You know, I was expecting you'd be back to see me," said Linden as he led me down to his basement. He took the steps a little faster than I did.

"You get the local paper, Homer?"

"Sure do. If you mean the *Calem Chronicle.*"

"The one with the 'Police Blotter.' "

He sat down on one of his machines, two-handedly swinging a towel over his head and onto his neck, like a jump rope. "Read it religiously. Just like I listen to the police radio." He thought a moment. "You're talking about Lainie now, aren't you?"

"That's right."

He wagged his head left to right. "Damn shame. God-damned judges don't realize that a man who'd break into a house just as soon kill somebody who surprised them."

"You figure that's how it happened."

"I was there. Afterwards, I mean. Heard the radio call on my scanner, got there just after Clay and Bjorkman. Walked around back with Bjorkman, saw the door and all."

"That would take care of any footprints the police might cast for comparison purposes."

Linden looked at me funny. "What do you mean?"

"I mean that your walking around there with old Georgie would bollix up any footprints you might have left there earlier."

Linden started to laugh, then stopped. "What the hell? You mean you think I killed her?"

"Maybe both."

"Both?"

"Both Jennifer and Lainie."

This time Homer did laugh. "Boy, you are putting me on."

"What makes you think so?"

Linden fixed me with a finger-shaking look. "Now, listen up. I was an investigator when you was still wetting yourself. Just guys tapping into other people's lines for billing diversion or getting their rocks off listening to their neighbors talk dirty to their lovers. But I still learned my trade, boy, and I'm thinking you haven't."

"Then show me where I'm going wrong."

"Well, let me give you opportunity, because I was there when Jennifer got shot and near enough when Lainie got bashed. How about means? Daniels used his own gun on Jennifer."

"He gave it to you."

"What?"

"You asked him for it and he gave it to you."

"Just like that?"

"Right."

"Fine. If that's your reasoning on this, I don't see we need to get to motive."

"Motive's easy too. You had the hots for Jennifer. She liked to 'experiment.' Maybe she decided a randy, well-conditioned old guy would be interesting."

"Boy, do you have any idea how crazy you sound?"

"Homer, don't you think it's just a little bit odd that two people from the same counseling group get killed four weeks apart?"

"Not as odd as you thinking I had something to do with it." He broke off. "Does seem funny that both of them got it, though."

"Especially since William could have killed only Jennifer."

"If William didn't kill Jennifer . . ."

"Then who did? And how, with William still having his gun? And if he didn't do it, then why did he confess to it?"

Homer rolled his lower lip down till it almost touched his chin. "If it wasn't William, how the hell . . . You said before that I could have killed Jennifer because William would have just given me the gun?"

"Yes."

"Why? Why would he have given it to me?"

"Like I said. Because you asked him."

Homer shook his head. "Boy, you make no sense at all."

"Bear with me, all right? I want to try something out on you."

Linden watched me warily. "All right," without enthusiasm.

"When you talked to the police, you said that you, Marek, Ramelli, and Lainie Bishop were waiting for William and Jennifer when William burst in, right?"

"That's right."

"Were all of you already in the meeting room?"

"Yeah."

"Did anything unusual happen before William entered?"

"What do you mean?"

"Did anyone act out of the ordinary?"

Homer sniffed. "Everybody in there was out of the ordinary. That's why they were there in the first place, you know?"

"I mean, did anybody, any of you four, do anything different than usual?"

"No. Well, it was unusual for anybody to be late, that was kind of a rule, otherwise we all got gypped out of some of our time, time with Marek, I mean. And it was especially odd that William was late."

"Why?"

"Well, for one thing, he was almost always there first. I suppose because he had the farthest of any of us to come."

"What do you mean?"

"Well, since it was bad to be late, and he lived so far away, I always figured he got there early so he wouldn't get stuck on a bus or something and hold the rest of us up."

"You said for one thing?"

"Huh?"

"You said that was one reason he wouldn't be late. Was there another?"

"Oh, yeah. It was his turn to be hypnotized. So he was really gypping himself most of all by not being there on time."

"Did anybody comment on that?"

"Comment?" Linden put his hands to the ends of the

towel and drew down alternately on it, like milking a cow in slow motion. "Let's see. Ramelli complained something about missing a Celtics play-off game—he has some kind of fancy sports cable hookup. Lainie looked like she always does, kind of moony at—Jesus, Lainie, I'm sorry. No need to be talking like that about you now."

"Moony at whom?"

"Marek. She had the . . . she thought he was attractive."

"Anything ever come of it?"

"Don't think so, but I'm not too good at guessing that kind of thing. She never let on that they did, and I think she would have, just by the way she'd talk or look, if it happened."

"You said she gave Marek a 'moony' look."

"Yeah, but it was, I dunno, more an 'I want you' than a 'wasn't it great' kinda look. You gotta remember, Lainie wasn't real subtle about that kind of thing usually."

"Meaning?"

"Meaning I think Lainie really felt something for him. Something more'n just physical."

"Did Jennifer feel the same way?"

"What, about Marek?"

"Yes."

Homer thought a minute before answering. "Not exactly. I'd say Jennifer looked at him more with—what did Jimmy Carter call it—'lust in the heart'?"

I remembered the super in Marek's building seeing Jennifer there much earlier than group session. "You have any evidence of it?"

Homer thought some more, scratched his head. "No."

"Back to that night, before William came in. Did Marek say anything?"

"I think all he said was maybe we should get started. And oh, yeah, he said Lainie should move."

"Lainie move?"

"Yeah. It was just because of the way we were sitting. We always took the same chairs every session. It's supposed to establish some kind of comforting environment for the one to be hypnotized. Well, Marek suggested Lainie should move because with Jennifer and William not being there, there were two seats empty between Marek and Lainie."

"I don't get it."

Linden got up. "Let me show you." He crossed to a cluttered little desk off in the corner and waded through some running magazines and time charts until he found a pad and pencil. He came back and sat down next to me. Though I assume he'd been exercising when I arrived, he had no body odor at all.

"This," he said, drawing, "is where Marek would sit. At the medicine table."

"I've seen it."

"And here are all our chairs. There are more chairs in the room than these, but that's because our group is a little smaller than some he runs. Anyway, here's the layout for us, and this is where each of us would sit if we weren't the one going under that night." Linden made little squares for each chair and wrote the first names of each member through his or her seat. He pointed to the two next to Marek. "These were William and Jennifer's, and he said to Lainie, 'Why don't you move over,' meaning closer to him. And she said, 'No, I'm fine where I am.' "

"Didn't you think that strange?"

"How so?"

"That Lainie, who was 'mooning' over Marek, didn't want to sit closer to him?"

"Well, she said no with that saucy look she has . . . had, so I figured it was just kind of her way of flirting with him, you know?"

"Marek ever ask anyone to move before?"

"I don't think so."

"What did Marek do when Lainie refused to change chairs?"

"He gave her one of his phony toothpaste smiles and just said something like, 'Well, why don't we all just talk, then,' and that's where William came in on us."

"Did Marek do anything different with William?"

"No. I mean, William was all hepped up about Jennifer. Course, we didn't know that then, but he was all jazzed up about something, so Marek tried to calm him down."

"Then Marek injected him?"

"That's right. But like I told you last time, it didn't seem to do much good."

I looked down at Linden's sketch. "Show me where Marek would stand when he gave the injection."

"Well, right here," said Homer, pointing in front of the center chair.

"So William, in the center chair, would have been between you and Marek."

"Right."

I paused for a minute. "And also between Ramelli and Marek."

"Squarely between Don and the doc, right."

"So you couldn't actually see Marek put the needle into William. And neither could Ramelli."

"Well, no, I guess not."

"I know this isn't to scale, but I want you to concentrate on the way it was that night in the meeting room. From Lainie's regular chair, could Marek have blocked her view of him injecting William?"

Linden looked down at the sketch, turned it to a different perspective, like a road map when you want to head south instead of north. "Hard to say for sure, but no, I don't think he could have."

"And if she had moved?"

"To the other chair, you mean?"

"Yes."

He studied it again. "Yeah, if she'd been in the other chair, he'd have been between her and William."

I stared at the sketch.

Homer said, "Boy, you okay?"

I looked up at him. "Sort of."

TWENTY-TWO

I left Linden's house with his sketch in my inside coat pocket. It was hours till Clay would come onto his tour, and I didn't feel like risking my tenuous relationship with O'Boy by pressing for Clay's home address. Then I reflected for a minute. Cops in Boston never list themselves in the phone book. No reason to invite harassing calls or twisted retribution. But maybe in Calem?

I found a pay phone and a directory for Boston Suburban West in a drugstore in the center of town. There were two Clays listed, both with first initials only. I couldn't remember if I had ever heard Clay's given name. Listing number one turned out to be a renter who'd never heard of Officer Clay. I tried number two.

"Hello?" said an older, female voice.

"Hello. My name is John Cuddy. I'm a detective from

Boston and I'm trying to reach a Calem police office named Clay."

"I'm afraid Harold's not listed in the phone book."

Harold. No wonder I hadn't heard Clay's first name before. "Is this Mrs. Clay?"

"Yes, I'm Harold's mother. Try him at the police station here. He'll be there a little before four this afternoon."

"I'm sorry, Mrs. Clay"—thinking back to something O'Boy said when I first met him—"but I tried the station already, and there's something wrong with the lines there. I found you by going through the directory."

"Oh, they've been having trouble with their phones for weeks. I'll tell you what, though. If you'll give me your number, I'll call my son and have him call you right back."

"It's important that I reach him as soon as possible."

"Well, the sooner you give me your number, the sooner you'll be able to speak with him."

I gave her the pay phone number.

"Why, that's our exchange. You're calling from here in Calem, aren't you?"

"Yes, ma'am."

"Then you could just as easily drive to the police station here and ask them, couldn't you?"

"Ma'am . . ."

"What did you say your name was again?"

"John Cuddy."

"You're not really a policeman, are you?"

"No, Mrs. Clay, I'm a private detective."

"And you thought you could trick me into giving you my son's number, didn't you?"

"Ma'am, I wasn't trying to trick—"

"Good day, Mr. Cuddy." She hung up.

I felt like a ten-year-old caught with a forged hall pass. I could see where Clay got his cop instincts.

I held down the receiver lever, got a dial tone, and called my service. A message from Mariah Lopez, giving me the name and telephone number of a professor at Boston University Medical School who was a hypnosis "buff." Also, a message from Sam Creasey, asking me to telephone him at the television station.

I hung up to call Creasey, but the pay phone rang before I could dial. I answered it.

"Hello?"

"You really are an asshole," said Harold Clay's voice.

"Can I explain?"

"First you job my partner, and then you try to jive my mother, and I'm—"

"Give me two minutes to explain, then you can hang up if you want. Okay?"

He didn't reply.

"Clay?"

"I'm looking at my watch."

I told him I'd spoken with Linden, tried to find his number in the directory, and reached his mother that way.

"So you figured I was stupid enough to maybe list my own phone number? And then you try to slide one past my mother?"

"I need the answers to a couple of questions. You've got every right to be pissed at me, both over what I said to Bjorkman and what I tried to do to your mother. My guess is that you would have done the same if you were in my position."

"Not for some ghetto stud who—" Clay stopped. "Sorry, that was George talking. Bjorkman, I mean. You ride with a guy for a while, you pick up parts of him."

179

"The night Jennifer was killed, you and Bjorkman responded."

"That's right. It's all in the report."

"Did you guys have William Daniels's blood tested for drugs?"

"No. Not George and me, that is. That would have been the detectives' side of it. Talk to O'Boy about it."

"When you and Bjorkman first saw Daniels, did you examine him in any way?"

"Examine him? We sure as hell braced him to see if he had any knives or other weapons."

"Did he appear drugged to you?"

"No. Look, I don't know what you're getting at here. He seemed completely in control of himself. No indication at all of being under the influence."

I tried to sound soothing. "I'm not trying to put him in for insanity. I just need to know. Did you look at his arms for tracks?"

"Black kid in this town? Sure, first thing I checked after we sat him back down."

"And?"

"Just the one fresh needle mark. A couple of other, faded ones, but the shrink—Marek—said those were from the other times the kid was under the stuff, the drug he gives them to loosen them up for hypnotizing."

"You looked at both arms?"

"Yes," he said, sounding impatient.

"And just one fresh mark."

"Yes. That do it?"

"Just two more questions."

"What are they?"

"Last night, at Lainie Bishop's house, could Homer Linden have gotten there by picking up your radio call?"

"Jesus, you'd have to hear the tape log to be sure, but

yeah, if he knew radio code he could figure out what happened. Her address would have come over in the clear."

"Has he ever responded to any other calls over the years that you know of?"

Clay said slowly, "Yeah. I can think of two. An armed robbery attempt at the liquor store and a fire, maybe half a mile from him."

"One last question."

"You said only two more a minute ago."

"I know, but this one will pin down something for me and save you and Bjorkman a lot of time. It may also piss you off even more at me."

"For chrissakes, ask it!"

"When you and Bjorkman swung onto the four-to-twelve shift yesterday, was he with you the whole time till Lainie Bishop was found dead?"

I was right about getting him madder. He hung up.

I tried Murphy, but he was out. I called Creasey's number, and got a secretary, who said he was in a meeting but had told her that if I called, he'd like me to have lunch with him at the television station. She sounded a little harried, so we quickly agreed on twelve noon.

I reached Dr. Douglas Kirby, the professor Mariah Lopez recommended, at his office. He said he could squeeze me in about three-thirty, if it wouldn't take too long. I assured him it wouldn't, hoping as I said it that his intrinsic interest in hypnosis would keep his eyes off the clock.

Creasey's station—or his wife's father's station, I guess—lay back from one of those two-lane roads that crisscross Route 128, the major high-tech beltway around Boston. The road had gotten too small to carry the computer commuters comfortably anymore, and I had to wait for a count of sixty and through a deafening barrage of horns from the people stopped behind me before I could make a left-hand turn into the driveway. I passed a utility van with the legend CHANNEL 8 NEWS/MOBILE UNIT #3. The van was parked at an angle on the edge of the parking lot, presumably to get the jump on a breaking story. I edged the Fiat into a VISITOR space and entered the building.

The reception area was disappointingly utilitarian. No autographed posters of anchor, sports, or weather personalities. The receptionist was a little short with me but buzzed a number. A middle-aged woman with the voice of Creasey's secretary fetched me two minutes later. She tried to make strained small talk as she led me to an elevator, up two floors, and down one corridor. There seemed to be people arguing behind at least two of the closed doors we passed. We stopped at an opened door.

"Is something the matter?" I said.

"The matter?"

"Yes. The atmosphere around here seems kind of uptight."

She tried to smile, but couldn't quite bring it off. "I'm sorry, it's just this licensing fight. They're really not being fair to Mr. Creasey. Especially after . . . well . . ." She changed tone and gestured into the room. "Please be comfortable. Mr. Creasey will be with you in a moment. Please don't smoke."

She left me. I felt as though I were entering the Calem Police interrogation room again.

The dining room was hardly ten by ten, with linoleum floor and bare painted walls. Centered on the floor were a table and chairs for four but place-set for only two. A small window let in some light but little atmosphere. There was one daffodil in a thin, plain glass vase at the center of the table. I began to get the feeling that the present manager was not a spendthrift.

I sat down, sipped at a glass of water. Creasey rushed in as I was putting the glass down.

He said, "Don't get up," but I did anyway and we shook.

"I'd offer you a drink, but I don't permit my employees to drink on the job, here or in the field, so I don't, either."

"Seems fair."

A waitress appeared seconds later with two cold deli plates, a small tray of assorted breads, and one iced tea with lemon.

"I don't take caffeine," he said.

"They make it without now," I said, sipping the tea. Strong.

"Yes, I know. I've tried it. It tastes . . . synthetic, unnatural. I don't like unnatural things."

"Well, why did you want to see me?"

"Would it be all right if we ate first? I've been going at it with the lawyers on this license mess since eight o'clock."

"Fine by me. I missed breakfast this morning."

We ate in silence. Granted he was more familiar with the limited menu than I was, but he didn't waste a motion, ingesting calories as if he had time only to take on necessary fuel, not taste the food as well.

He finished way ahead of me and seemed not to know quite what to do with himself. I half expected him to call for a report and catch up on his reading.

I laid my knife and fork on the plate at ten-past-two position and downed the last of my iced tea. "Ready when you are."

"I like you, John. Enough that I want to trust you."

"I like you too, Mr. Creasey—I'm sorry, Sam—but not quite enough to trust you."

He smiled and almost seemed to relax. He pushed his

plate to the side of the table. The waitress appeared un-bidden to clear the table, leaving only the daffodil and our water glasses and refilling the latter.

He got serious again as soon as she closed the door behind her. "You believe that Jennifer's murder and the death of Lainie Bishop last night are connected, don't you?"

"Yes, but remember, it would be in my client's interest to believe that."

"Because?"

"Because if they're connected in the sense that the same person committed both, then William is innocent because he couldn't have killed Lainie from his jail cell."

"Agreed. I've been thinking over what you said to me in your car. About inconsistencies and so on."

"Anything more to add?"

"I'm not sure, but Pina . . . she's our maid?"

"I remember her."

"Well, Jennifer had been living at home for the last few weeks, and not because she preferred Tyne and me to the dormitory. Pina believes that the McCatty boy was both-ering her at school."

"And therefore?"

"And therefore maybe he was the one."

"Who set William up, you mean?"

"Yes. I even remember Jennifer talking once at dinner about hypnosis and how McCatty had learned how to do it."

"Learned how to put people under?"

"Exactly."

"So does Bjorkman."

"He does?"

"From the police academy. Linden too."

"Linda?"

184

"No, Homer Linden. He's an older man from Jennifer's psychotherapy group."

Creasey ground his jaw. "It would have been like Jennifer to . . . approach an older man."

I had been rolling a question around in my mind for a while. Sam was the only one other than Deborah Wald I thought might know the answer to it, and after what she'd been through with her father, I wasn't about to call her about it.

"Sam, I want to ask you a question. I'm not looking forward to it, but it might help me."

"Ask it."

I rested both my hands flat on the table, separated by about the width of Creasey's shoulders. I said, "Did Jennifer ever approach you?"

He threw his left at my face before he even started to stand up. I flicked my right up and parried it. He stood, and I followed him up as he swung his right at me. I took it on my left forearm as the table went over, the vase and water glasses smashing on the floor.

Creasey seemed distracted by the shattering noise. He bent over to the flower. I said, "Don't cut yourself."

He muttered something to himself and stood back up. "I'm sorry." He didn't appear to want to hit me anymore. He righted the table and the chairs it carried over with it. "Please," he said, gesturing for me to sit as he did.

I sat back down. He looked out the window and talked softly.

"It was just before Christmas. Tyne was in New York. She goes there every year to do holiday shopping. I got home late from one of those sports banquets where they raise money for some good cause. I can't even remember. . . . Anyway, I was sitting next to a former Red Sox player I admired when I first moved here. He was quite a drinker and . . . well, I'm not. But I stayed with him at and after this dinner for a few rounds. Then I drove home. Jennifer heard me come in.

"I heard her coming down the stairs. I called to her. 'Playfully,' she said later. I'm not a 'playful' man, John. But I was feeling good and so I called to her, said how are you doing, how come a beautiful girl like you isn't out, and so on. It was the liquor. My back was still to her as I dropped my coat and briefcase on a chair. Then she said, 'You sound playful tonight. Well, I feel playful too.' That was when I turned around. She . . ." Creasey swallowed hard. "She had on just a bra and panties. She swayed over to me. I was too . . . stunned to move or say anything. She reached up here"—he poked his tie at his breastplate—"and unsnapped her bra. It . . . they just fell open and then she slipped her arms around my neck, and kissed me hard and open. Her mouth, I mean. I . . . I came to my senses and pushed her away, harder than I had to. She banged into a small stand near the wall and knocked over a vase. An expensive one, a wedding present from one of Tyne's aunts. It fell and broke and Jennifer ran away, up the stairs, cursing at me. 'I thought you wanted to play,' she said, over and over, as she ran up the stairs. 'I thought you wanted to play.' "

Creasey swallowed hard, closed his eyes. "That's it."

"You tell your wife about this?"

He shook his head. "Didn't have to. Jennifer did. Locked herself in her room, called her mother in New York, and said I'd gotten drunk and attacked her. I was outside Jennifer's door. She screamed at me to get on another extension, that Tyne wanted to talk to me. I went into our bedroom and picked up the receiver. Tyne was— I think she'd been drinking some too—Tyne was hysterical, calling me all sorts of names, threatening to call the police. It was a nightmare."

He raised his face to me, then leaned halfway across the table. He really did look a lot like Gregory Peck. In the crack-up scene from *Twelve O'Clock High.*

He said, "Now you see why I've got to know the police have the right one. The one who really killed her."

I said, "Yes, I do," even though I didn't have the slightest idea what he meant.

TWENTY-THREE

As I walked back to my car in the Channel 8 parking lot, I decided that I had enough time before my appointment with Professor Kirby to pay a visit to Dr. Marek. The drive took fifteen minutes in the hurry-scurry traffic that seems always to crowd suburban areas on Friday afternoons.

I parked in front of Marek's building and entered the lobby. I walked downstairs to the basement, answering some time and distance questions I had. I also tried to find my friend the maintenance man, but he must have been off at another of the owner's properties, "saving a dime." I climbed the stairs all the way to Marek's floor.

His receptionist was typing on some short-form stationery as I came through the door. Given what I guessed Marek's rates were, I would have thought he'd at least send out his bills on full-sized paper. She looked up with a practiced smile, not quite placing me. "Can I help you?"

"I hope so. I don't have an appointment, but I was here on Tuesday, and I think Dr. Marek would really appreciate hearing what I've found out since then."

"Let me . . . I'm sorry, I've forgotten your . . ."

"Cuddy, John Cuddy. I'm sure Dr. Marek will remember me."

She worked hard to keep quizzical from hardening into disapproving. "Please be seated. I'll tell him you're here." She stood and made her way to and through the doorway to his office while I busied myself with the periodicals on his waiting area table. Sandwiched between last month's issue of *Town & Country* and this month's issue of *Ducks Unlimited* was a copy of a recent *Calem Chronicle*.

She reappeared in the doorway and said, "The doctor will see you now."

I said thank you and passed her as she moved back to the bills.

Marek was sitting at his desk, laying down a dictating microphone and adjusting some dial on a control panel as I sat down.

"Well, Mr. Cuddy, good to see you again," he said without looking up. He finally finished with the control panel and actually engaged me. "Unfortunately, I need Friday afternoons to catch up on correspondence and such, so I'm afraid that I can't give you much time. Mrs. Porter said that you had something important to tell me?"

Nicely done. Parameters of interview set, warm inflection on last clause to encourage me to state my news succinctly, with little time for discussion.

"Actually, I thought you might be in need of a little counseling yourself today."

He canted his head toward a shoulder. "I'm not sure I . . ."

"Lainie Bishop was killed last night."

189

"Yes, tragic. I heard it on the late news."

"Kind of an epidemic."

"Epidemic?"

"Among your patients, I mean. First Jennifer, then William, as a consequence anyway, and now Lainie."

"I don't think . . . The news bulletin suggested a burglar, I believe."

"And therefore how could Jennifer and Lainie be connected?"

"Well, yes."

"Doctor, doesn't it strike you as at least peculiar that the ranks of your patients are thinning out so quickly and specifically?"

"I'm afraid I'm finding this conversation a bit obtuse, Mr. Cuddy. What do you mean by 'specifically'?"

"That two members of a five-person therapy group are murdered within a month of each other and a third member is charged on one of them. Doesn't that seem kind of selective to you?"

"But it's clear that William killed Jennifer and that he couldn't have killed Lainie. And Lainie's death seems certain to have been due to some startled prowler. Aside from mere coincidence, I don't see the connection."

"I notice that you get the *Chronicle.*"

"The local paper, you mean?"

"Yes."

"What of it?"

"Do you read the 'Police Blotter' column?"

He gave me a tolerant smile. "Not my favorite."

"Too bad. I hear it covers local crime waves pretty thoroughly. Like the string of burglaries before Lainie was killed."

Marek shook his head, then looked down toward his microphone. "Really, Mr. Cuddy. I don't understand what you're driving at, and I do have a mountain of work yet to move today, so . . .''

"It must be kind of lonely for you on Thursdays now."

"What?"

"Without the experimental group, I mean."

"Mr. Cuddy, I fail to see . . ."

"Of course, it also frees up your time for other things."

"What are you insinuating?"

"Like house calls, for example."

"I think you'd better leave, sir."

I peeked down at my watch. "Gee, thanks. I do have another appointment. I'm going to see somebody about hypnosis. I understand it can be a very helpful device." I stood up and moved toward the door. "By the way, Doctor, did Jennifer ever tell you what a crush she had on you?"

When I looked back at Marek, he was giving me the tolerant smile again. "Do close the door and please don't bother me after today. Understood?"

If I was right about Marek, I had to admire his recovery ability. If I was wrong about him, I wasn't sure where else to look.

The drive into the city was pleasant, the afternoon warm and sunny. It helped that the first outriders of the rush-hour traffic were coming at me rather than traveling with me. I wound my way to the medical school's South End location, a good distance from Boston University's main campus on Commonwealth Avenue. I parked in an illegal space and walked to a four-story building.

Professor—Doctor—Douglas Kirby was a happy surprise. He was bright, knowledgeable, and he tactfully ignored the passing of about an hour and a half. We discussed flurazepam and placebos, suppression states and nightmares. Especially as they related to the force of hypnosis and posthypnotic suggestions. I left his office with five books under my arm.

I spent the balance of Friday night and most of Saturday at home reading the material Kirby had lent me. I grew pretty certain of the who and the how of Jennifer's death. What I still didn't know was the why. And with Lainie dead, I wasn't likely to uncover that without getting on at least one plane. I called Murphy and Mrs. Daniels, advising them what I was going to do. They insisted on footing the bills, and I declined by hanging up on each. I then reached my landlord in Chicago, who said that although she was at a different hospital, she would personally call Dr. Jerome Gemelman and ask him to see me on Monday. She was going out of town to a conference, so she also gave me the name and telephone numbers of an administrative dean at a Chicago law school whom she knew and who might be able to help if I ran into any snags. "Jim's a little weird, John, but he's good." I thanked her and wondered briefly, before I made my airline and hotel reservations, how weird a dean at a law school could be.

TWENTY-FOUR

I got up at 8:00 A.M. on that cloudy Sunday morning and thought about packing my running gear for the trip. Instead, I put it on and ran a slow but satisfying six-mile loop from the condo west to and across the Harvard Square bridge and then east along the Cambridge side of the river before crossing back over at the Mass Ave bridge. I bought the Sunday *Times* and some croissants and milk, then walked home and showered. While my hair dried, I ate breakfast, skimmed the *Times*, and filled a carry-on case. I dressed casually, called a cab, and headed to the airport. With one intermediate stop.

"You gonna be here long, Mac?"

I shook my head. "Ten minutes, maybe. Leave the meter running."

"Don't worry, I will. Freaking cemeteries give me the creeps, y'know?"

"Yeah, me too."

The sun was just breaking through the overcast as I drew even with her stone. The rays made her name on it wink at me. "That's a pretty good trick, kid."

Practice, she said. *Where are you going?*

"Chicago, then maybe on to Philadelphia and New York."

See America first?

"Not exactly. I took your advice. I assumed that William didn't kill Jennifer and then tried to see who could have set him up. Any alternative killer was helped most by William spilling the beans at the hypnosis session. Probably the only one with both the opportunity and the ability to set that up was Dr. Marek himself, since he was the one who could control the hypnosis session."

But I thought he didn't seem to have a motive.

"He didn't. And doesn't. But there's some indication that Jennifer was interested in him romantically. Unfortunately, there's no real proof of it, and the doctor was very good at covering his emotions if anything ever came of it. The only person around who seems to have been Jennifer's confidante was killed Thursday."

How?

"Made to look like an interrupted burglary, but my guess is the confidante drew some conclusions from whatever Jennifer told her and then confronted Marek, or somebody else, with them."

Which is why you're going to Chicago?

"Yeah. That's the last place before Boston that Marek worked. He also worked in Philly and New York. I'm working my way backward through his career, betting that if he had something going with a female patient here, he may have a history of it somewhere else."

Which would give him a motive to kill Jennifer?

"I grant you, not much of a motive in this day and age, I suppose. But right now I don't have anything else. And William's got nothing."

He's got you.

The cabbie honked twice. I looked over at him and nodded.

Rude guy, she said.

"He doesn't like cemeteries."

So stiff him on the tip.

"No pun intended?"

We laughed and said good-bye.

O'Hare Airport might be bigger than the town in which you grew up. I remembered having to fly in and out of there maybe six times in my days at Empire Insurance. The terminals are designed so that every gate is at least three miles from its airline's corresponding ticket counters when you're departing and from the baggage carousels when you're arriving. I carried my bag outside and waited on the taxi line for nearly an hour as a dispatcher of some kind filled only one cab at a time. Most of the travelers around me seemed resigned to the system, so I didn't see the sense in complaining. When my turn came, I just climbed into the rear seat and told the back of the driver's head, "The Raphael Hotel, please. On East Delaware off Michigan."

He said, "You bet."

I settled back into the seat, looked up at the cab's roof, and saw a glossy eight-by-ten autographed photo of Nat King Cole. Except it wasn't Cole.

"That's me," said the cabbie, adjusting his inside rearview mirror so that I could see his face.

It was uncanny. The features, the hair, even the easy, relaxed smile.

"I'm a professional impersonator. I just drive the cab between gigs." He reached into the glove compartment and passed me a recent copy of *Newsweek*. "That's me there, up at the head table." I could barely make him out, along with four others, seated at a table on a stage and looking down at an auditorium containing several hundred burly white men wearing white T-shirts and sporting bald heads. "They asked me to judge the Mr. Clean contest."

"How did you get started in all this?"

"Well, when I was growing up, my family saw the resemblance. Then I entered one of these celebrity lookalike contests and came in third, and that was without any . . . they call it 'cosmetic advantage.' "

"Meaning surgery?"

"No. That is, not for me. I've heard some of the Elvis impersonators have done that, but my bone structure and all were already okay. I just needed some teeth capped and a little work on my hairline is all."

"And what do you do? Photographic modeling?"

"Yeah, yeah. Some of that. A lot of us have this agent here in town who sets that stuff up. I do parties sometimes too. You know, the host'll get in touch with my agent ahead of time and like hire three or four different lookalikes. Then we come to the party and just mingle with the guests and the host gets a kick out of the way they react to us. Course, I don't do all that many parties."

"How come?"

He shrugged. "Some folks think it's kind of weird having a dead celebrity walk up to them with a drink in his hand, you know?"

"I guess I can see that."

"Yeah, so it's the live ones that get the most party gigs, like the Queen Elizabeths and the Michael Jacksons and so on."

I was hesitant to ask him about his voice, but I didn't have to.

"That's why my agent has me taking singing lessons. The real money for this stuff is in putting on a nightclub act, say maybe three of us each doing a set, you know, like a Bing Crosby and me wrapped around maybe a Jack Benny. Of course, I never . . ." He looked up in the mirror at me, then continued, "Were you old enough to remember his TV show?"

"Cole's?"

"Yeah."

"You bet." In the mid-fifties, the King was the first black I recalled having really his own program, not counting the stereotypical situation comedies like *Beulah* and *Amos and Andy*. On a nondescript gray stage setting, Cole would introduce his guests, play his piano, and sing his songs, all with an effortless grace under what must have been the incredible pressure of being both the first and the only.

"I wish I could have seen that. But I got a few of his TV spots from later on tape, and I'm really trying to get his mannerisms down. My voice won't ever be close to his, but if I can get my head to tilt right and my hands to work right . . ." The cabbie gave a sort of half wave with his right hand, the way I thought Cole signed off his programs. "Well, they say if you can get the mannerisms, the people, y'know, the audience like, they'll hear what they want to hear, and they'll leave happy because of me being able to do that."

"Sounds like you can justify your job a lot better than most guys I know."

"Thanks."

We pulled up to the Raphael. I tipped him five dollars on a twenty-dollar fare, and we wished each other luck.

As I checked in, the desk clerk offered me the literature on the other Raphaels, which I already had. There are only three in the chain, and I had stayed only at this one and the one in San Francisco. If the Kansas City entry is as well run and well located as the other two, the Raphael family should be making a well deserved fortune.

I was shown to my room, mixed a screwdriver from the honor-system stocked bar and refrigerator, and flopped on the king-sized bed. I decided to call Jim, the law school dean, just to let him know I was in town. I punched what I'd been given as Jim's home phone number.

After three rings, a voice answered, "City Morgue."

"I'm sorry, I must have dialed the wrong—"

"Hold on, hold on. Is this Karen's friend from Boston?"

"Yes, is this—"

"Yup, it's me. I thought I recognized the accent. We get a few Boston-area people coming out here to school. Where are you staying?"

"The Raphael. I—"

"Hey, nice place. Karen said you were a runner?"

"Just to stay in shape. Listen—"

"Did you bring your running gear?"

"No, I didn't. I'm just going to be here today and tomorrow."

"Oh, no. That doesn't give me much time."

"Time?"

"Yeah. To show you the city. Chicago, my adopted homeland."

"Listen—"

"I'm from Toledo, originally. What're you doing this afternoon?"

"I just got in and I thought I'd—"

"Well, look. I've got to go set something up at the school for this afternoon, but I'll be free by five—no, by four-thirty. Meanwhile, you . . . Do you like museums?"

In spite of myself, I thought back to Beth and me roving through the Boston Museum of Fine Arts and realized I hadn't been there since she'd died. "Yes."

"Great. There's a terrific exhibit called the Treasury of San Marco at the Art Institute of Chicago. Just down the street—Michigan Avenue, that is—from where you are now. Just tell a cabdriver to take you there. It's at the corner of Adams, maybe a three-buck ride each way. You'll love it. Then I'll be by your hotel to pick you up at four-thirty. Wear something you won't mind getting stained."

"What?"

"You can't miss my car. It's a Rabbit that looks like a square pumpkin. See you then. Gotta run. Bye."

I sat on the bed, stared at the phone, and finished my drink.

The Art Institute looked the part from the outside. A massive, apparently granite building with a broad set of steps flanked by two impressive but greened-over bronze lions. There was a long but courteous line of people waiting to buy tickets for the San Marco exhibit. I paid my $4.50 and was gently ushered along with them into a veiled room of splendor.

The exhibit consisted of maybe fifty display cases, set off individually with enough vertical electronic security cables to discourage a remake of *Topkapi*. All four sides of each case had identical plaques, briefly explaining the

199

treasure within the glass enclosure. Most of the items were renderings of communion chalices and other religious artifacts in gold, enamel, and jewels. As I wound my way through the labyrinth of hanging cloth and indirect lighting, a number of things struck me. Most amazing was the quality of the craftsmanship, including a number of crystalline vessels from the tenth and eleventh centuries. Most unfortunate was the inescapable conclusion that the Treasure of San Marco was really the spoils of the sack of Constantinople, carried back to a persuasive pope by somewhat overzealous crusaders.

I spent the balance of the afternoon at the museum wandering through some East Asian, architectural, and photographic galleries. I'd forgotten how enjoyable that could be, and I grudgingly admitted I'd have to thank my maniacal substitute host for suggesting it.

It did look like a square pumpkin.

"Hey, how are you?"

I shook his hand and climbed in. "I'm fine and the museum was great."

Jim pumped his head and ground his gears. "Yeah, Karen and I saw it last week and loved it. The crusaders ever hit this town, there won't be a slice of bread left on the shelves. You know much about Chicago?"

"Not really."

That was all he needed.

We covered neighborhoods, transportation, politics, universities, restaurants . . .

"And this," he said, doing a U-turn to catch an opposite-side empty parking space, "is like a memorial to dead brain cells everywhere." He pointed to the sign over a tavern door, THE ULTIMATE SPORTS BAR AND GRILL.

Erect and walking, Jim was about an inch taller than I.

He had shortish black hair, a beard, and a brow that shrouded his eyes so that you weren't immediately sure where he was looking at any given time. He was wearing tattered running shoes, baggy olive-drab fatigue pants, and a river boatman's collarless long-sleeved shirt. He was not what you'd call a slave to fashion, and I could imagine him helping to run a law school about as easily as I could imagine me piloting a spaceship.

"You're gonna love this place," he said over his shoulder as he led me in.

Jim saved my nodding head from being taken off as he caught a basketball humming on a bullet pass six feet off the ground.

"Oh, sorry, Jim," said somebody.

"No problem," he replied, dribbling the ball toward the side wall. The management had hung a basket and then encased the shooting approach to it in a clear plastic sleeve. The effect was that a person could launch foul shots at the rim and the sleeve would control and channel the ball, swish or rebound, back down the sleeve to the shooter.

As Jim approached the foul line, a bartender called out, "Seven in a row wins a free pitcher of house tap."

Jim acknowledged the challenge, took his stance, and sank twelve in a row before he said we needed a drink.

We stayed there about two hours, watching a late Cubs day game from the coast on the eight overhead TVs. We moved around the several drinking and eating areas, including a mock elevated boxing ring with cocktail tables and chairs inside it, as Jim introduced me to friends and acquaintances of his. It was the best bar afternoon I'd spent since the army, and I said so.

Jim smiled. "Tip of the iceberg. You getting hungry?"

I said yes, and he said let's go.

The next place was called the Twin Anchors, a more

neighborhood place. It had one long bar and an informal dining area in the rear. Jim walked up to the head waitress.

She said, "At least half an hour for a table, Jim."

Jim said, "But I have my friend here from Boston, and I've been telling him all day what great food you've got, and—"

"And it's still half an hour."

Suddenly Jim doubled over and said, "Beat me, whip me, make me write bad checks . . ."

"All right, all right. Enough, okay?" She blew out a breath, looked to me. "You know that's one of his routines, right? You know I'm saving you and me both at least twenty minutes of shtick, right?"

Before I could say anything, she looked behind her and said to Jim. "There's a table open next to the kitchen. Probably nobody else'd want it anyway." Then she smiled. "Connie's having a shaky night. Maybe she'll spill something on you."

As she got us menus, Jim turned to me and said, "That woman is one of the many reasons I love this town."

We gorged ourselves on barbecued baby back ribs, french fries, and Heileman's Old Style beer. Between watching him in the bar and talking to him over dinner, I could see why Jim would be a popular and effective administrator. Bright and well-informed, he was the rare storyteller who knew the value of listening appreciatively to other people's stories.

As I was using a Handi Wipe on my fingers, Jim said, "You like comedy? Improv stuff?"

"Yes."

"We're outta here."

I insisted on paying the check for dinner. Jim insisted he'd make it up later.

As we drove, he said, "This is Old Town. It was pretty

rough until a few years ago, when the gentrification started. Now it's getting pretty trendy, but this place has always been great."

He pointed to a red-brick building with a red and white flag as we parked across the street. The flag said THE SECOND CITY.

"Is this the place the *Saturday Night Live* people came from?"

"And then some. C'mon, I've got a friend in the group."

We walked into the building and up the stairs. While Jim arranged for tickets through his friend, I walked along the rogues' gallery of former members of the troupe. It was truly incredible. Mike Nichols and Elaine May, Jack Burns and Avery Schreiber, John Belushi, Bill Murray, Betty Thomas from *Hill Street Blues*, George Wendt from *Cheers*, and a dozen other familiar faces from over the years.

Jim said behind me, "Show's about to start."

We went into a raised cabaret room that seated maybe three hundred people around a small, bare stage. There were six people in the company, according to Jim always four men and two women. The cast members would rotate out when a new opportunity presented itself, but rarely would they return. That night they did six rehearsed skits, all of them ridiculous, tasteless, and screamingly funny. Then two of them came back out, soliciting from the audience simple phrases, like "Tupperware" and "city bus" and "Chicago Bears." Half an hour later, all six members were back, doing improvisational skits based on the audience suggestions. Watching them playing off and building on each other's inventiveness, you had to concede that the funniest person you ever knew would appear pretty amateurish next to them.

At the end of the show, the cast got a thunderous, stomping ovation. Jim asked me if I'd like to meet them, but I declined, preferring to keep the image of them I already had.

As we were filing out with the rest of the audience, I said to Jim, "You know, I don't want to keep you out too late."

He said, "You're just seeing some doctor tomorrow, right? I mean, you're not performing surgery or anything yourself?"

"That's right."

"Great."

I remember the names of some of the places we stopped. Gamekeepers, P. S. Chicago, Yvette's, a pizza place called Ranalli's with lots of imported beers and ales. Mostly, though, I remember just images, like the contours of a leather chair or the earrings a barmaid wore or the railing on the half-flight of stairs down to the men's room.

I do recall Jim's dropping me off back at the Raphael, the doorman coming to help me out of the car. Jim stuffed a piece of paper in my shirt pocket and said, "Be sure to call me tomorrow if you need help."

I leaned up against the doorman and turned back to the car to say thanks. Jim yelled something and drove off.

The doorman steadied me into the lobby. I asked him if he'd caught the last thing Jim said.

The doorman worked his mouth. "I believe, sir, he said something like 'Most fun I've had with my clothes on.' "

Probably verbatim.

TWENTY-FIVE

The fire alarm brought me up, legs churning, head whipping around madly, trying to spot clothes and shoes. Then I realized that I was still in them. My head began pounding, and the alarm noise began to sound too lengthy for the pauses in between. The telephone. Idiot. Hung-over idiot.

I picked up the receiver and said, "John Cuddy."

"Thought you might be in need of a wake-up call." Jim's voice.

"Thanks. What time is it anyway?"

"About seven-thirty A.M. Central Time. Anything you need?"

"Yeah. An Excedrin the size of a Hershey bar."

"Hah. You're just out of practice. Five days in this town'd make a new man out of you."

"How long should it take me to get to Chicago Memorial?"

"By cab, maybe twenty minutes with traffic. It's only a couple of blocks from where you were yesterday at the Art Institute."

"Good. I'll pull myself together and get down there. Thanks again for last night."

"No problem. I put my telephone numbers in your pocket again as you were getting out of the car. Call if you need me."

"I will."

I hung up, stripped, and took four aspirin with as many glasses of water. After I showered and shaved, I called Dr. Gemelman's office. His secretary said he was expecting me at ten o'clock, seventh floor, room 712. I thanked her, than marshaled my courage and went downstairs to the restaurant, forcing an order of French toast into the acid pit where once my stomach lay.

A different doorman whistled me a cab, and we pulled up in front of Chicago Memorial fifteen minutes later. The structure was old and looked more like a decaying office building than a hospital.

The sign to the right of Dr. Gemelman's door said ADMINISTRATIVE CHIEF. I walked in, gave my name to his secretary, and was shown into his inner office immediately.

She said, "Dr. Gemelman? Mr. Cuddy," and closed the door behind her as she left.

Gemelman rose, shook my hand, and waved me to a chair. He was maybe six one, skinny, with a high forehead, bushy eyebrows, and very hairy hands. His facial expression as he spoke suggested he had the personality of a rainy Tuesday night. "A Dr. Karen Barzlay asked me to see you, but she was vague as to why."

I smiled as ingratiatingly as possible. "I'm a private investigator from Boston. I'm helping an attorney there

defend a college student accused of murdering his girlfriend. The student and the girlfriend were members of a
therapy group run by a psychiatrist who used to work here.
I was wondering if you could give me some information
about him."

Gemelman frowned. "Information about the psychiatrist, you mean?"

"Yes."

"If I had known that was your purpose in seeing me, I
could have saved you a trip. We don't release that sort of
information, I'm afraid."

"I wouldn't necessarily need his file, Doctor. Just some
information about him, if you remember."

"I'm sorry; quite impossible."

I stopped for a minute, watching him.

"Mr. Cuddy, if there's nothing else . . ."

"Why the closed door, Doctor?"

"It's a matter of confidentiality, you see."

"No, I don't see. I'm not asking to see his patients'
files. I'm asking about him as an employee. What's so
confidential about that?"

"It is our policy not to discuss the employment records
of any of our physicians."

"Doctor, forgive me, but you can't be serious. I mean,
you must get credit inquiries, background checks from
other licensing states or organizations . . ."

"For which we require a prior release signed by the
physician involved. I can assure you we have none such
from Dr. Marek."

"Doctor, there is a murder involved here."

"I'll take your word for that."

"There is some evidence that the dead girl may have
sought a nonprofessional relationship with Marek."

"Mr. Cuddy, I have already explained our position. I'm sorry I can't help you."

"Are you going to force me to get the lawyer in Boston to begin proceedings out here?"

Gemelman frosted over. "We do not respond well to bluffs or threats, sir. We do respond to court orders properly issued. Feel free to pursue that course if you please. But now, if you don't mind . . ."

I rose. "Thanks for your time, Doctor."

I left his office and stopped near his secretary's desk to tie my shoelace. Her internal phone line buzzed. She picked it up, seemed to interrupt the caller by saying, "Oh, but he's still . . ." then simply said, "Yes, yes," several times while avoiding my gaze. I was pretty sure that she was being told by Gemelman to issue an incommunicado decree regarding me to the rest of the staff. I decided I ought to ask my landlord Karen if she ever mentioned Marek's name to Gemelman. I was pretty sure I hadn't told her his name, and I was damn sure I hadn't mentioned it to Gemelman before he'd used it himself.

I called Jim from a public phone in the lobby. He said that most hospitals in the city were tight with information, especially when there might have been something nobody wanted to reveal. He said I'd need a lot more legalese on paper before a judge in Chicago would order one of its own to open up. I thanked him and said I might be back to him, but I doubted it. He asked if he could show me some more of the town that night, but I told him I had to leave. He promised to let me reciprocate if he ever got to Boston. He also said he'd have Karen call me about the matter when she got back from her conference.

I cabbed to the hotel, my insides not quite up to lunch yet. I called United and got my ticket changed to an earlier flight. I packed up, checked out, and was driven to O'Hare by someone who looked like nobody famous. I was on the ground in Philadelphia by 3:00 P.M. Eastern Time and in front of Philadelphia Lutheran Hospital on City Line Avenue by 4:00 P.M.

I should have stayed in Chicago.

The administrative physician was on vacation. His secretary, a blond young woman with the complexion and shape of a Bartlett pear, told me that such information was not available without the permission of the subject or the direction of the secretary's absent superior. My use of the name Clifford Marek brought a cough and a sidesaddle smile, more reaction, I thought, than recalling the name only from a pink telephone message should have produced. I tried to pry some information from that opening, but the secretary knew both her job and a con job when she heard one. I left her and went back downstairs.

I thought about continuing on to New York then, but as I went backward through Marek's career I was losing ground, and heart along with it. Instead, I checked into a cut-rate motel near the hospital and next to a mini-mall on City Line. Thanks to the previous night with Jim, dinner consisted of a bland deli sandwich, two pieces of Drake's Pound cake, and a quart of milk.

TWENTY-SIX

Considering time and distance to the respective airports, it is easier to travel from Philadelphia to New York by train than by plane. I caught the Amtrak Narragansett from Thirtieth Street Station at 8:30 A.M. and pulled into Penn Station at 10:20. Given my luck so far, I left my bag in a locker and took a taxi to New York Central Hospital.

True to its name, the hospital building was located just off Central Park South. The exterior wore that dingy look that all but recently completed structures in the Big Apple seem to have. The interior, peeling linoleum floors and matching paint, was no improvement. The directory said I would find Psychiatric Services on the ninth floor.

There was a counter just off the elevator bank. The people behind it were dressed in no particular uniform. A thirtyish black male with hip-hugger pants and a carica-tured lisp asked if he could help me.

"I'm a private investigator from Boston, and I'd like some information about a doctor who used to work here."

"Well, anyone who's come that kind of distance ought to get all the help I can give. What's the doctor's name?"

"Clifford Marek."

The man stiffened, then crossed his arms. "I've worked in this office for eleven years and that kind of information is not available without the doctor's authorization or Ms. Smith's approval."

"Who's Ms. Smith?"

He swiveled around, pointing to a barely readable plaque on a closed door behind the counter. "The boss."

"Look, I'm not trying to be a wise-ass, but I've been chasing this thing for a couple of thousand miles now. Can I speak to Ms. Smith and explain things to her?"

"Certainly. Your name, please?"

I told him and he walked to the door, knocked, and waited. He frowned impatiently, knocked again, then opened the door and disappeared inside. He emerged a minute later leading a thickset middle-aged woman with a no-nonsense look to her.

"Mr. Cuddy, is it?" she said.

"Yes."

"Come in. Suley, hold my calls."

"Yessam," he said, derision in his voice.

I walked through the opening in the counter and into Ms. Smith's office. She indicated a seat for me and then plopped decisively into her own chair. "Now, what's this all about?"

I told her, including names and places.

She shook her head. "I can't release any such information about Dr. Marek."

"Ms. Smith—"

"Mr. Cuddy, either you obtain the doctor's authorization or a court order. We simply can't give out that kind of information otherwise. Every administrative superior in this hospital will back me on that."

"Tell me, does this insistence on procedures get triggered just by Dr. Marek's name?"

"I don't know what you mean."

"I mean that every time this particular man is mentioned in a hospital setting, everyday reasonable people go immediately bureaucratic on me." I regretted my choice of words before the last one was out of my mouth. You don't call a bureaucrat a bureaucrat and hope to receive any cooperation.

She buttoned up and stood up. "Have a nice day, Mr. Cuddy."

"Thanks. You too."

I let myself out of her office and walked toward the opening in the counter.

"Oh, Mr. Cuddy," said Suley, extending a folded piece of paper to me.

"Yes?"

"You dropped this on the way in to Ms. Smith."

I looked down at his hand. "I don't—"

"You did," he said, pushing the paper toward me. "I saw you."

"Thanks," I said, taking it from him.

He arched an eyebrow and said, "Glad to help," then returned to some other documents on the counter.

I waited until I was in the elevator before opening the paper. In ornate handwriting, it read: "Talk to Agnes Zerle, somewhere on the Boulevard in West New York. Tell her Diana Ross sent you. If Smith finds out, I'm blackened dogfish."

I smiled, refolded the note, and stuck it in my pocket.

* * *

"You mean New Jersey, pal," said the cabbie.

"No, I was told West New York."

"Yeah, but West New York is in New Jersey. Like a town there, get it?"

"Not exactly. How far is it?"

"Maybe ten miles. You'd be better off taking a bus."

"Where can I catch one?"

"Port Authority. Eighth and Forty-first. You wanna go there?"

"Please."

It was a short hop to the Port Authority building. I found a telephone book that had Ms. Zerle listed. I got no answer. I copied down her address and unsuccessfully asked some people where I could get a bus for West New York. After fending off two incredibly aggressive panhandlers, I found a ticket window for New Jersey Transit and bought a round-trip ticket on the number 165 local, departing platform 62. I found the platform up several nonconnecting flights of stairs and got on a huge, air-conditioned bus with contiguous lines of orange, lavender, and blue as racing stripes along the side. The bus was crowded, and I sat next to a dark-featured man reading a newspaper in what I believed were Arabic characters. From what I could hear around me, about half the passengers spoke Spanish.

We crawled through the Lincoln Tunnel to New Jersey and through several mazes of over- and underpasses. Then we began driving along a high, wide road paralleling the Hudson River, on the right and several hundred feet down. At the first stop, I noticed a street sign that said BOULE-VARD EAST. I left my seat and took one across from the driver.

"I want number sixty-three fifteen on the boulevard."

"In West New York?"

"Right."

"We got a ways to go yet. I'll let you know."

"Thanks."

I watched the view of the river and the New York sky-line across it, alternately spectacular and obstructed, depending upon whether someone had built a massive condominium between the cliff and the road. I could recognize only the twin towers of the World Trade Center, the Empire State Building, and the Citicorp Building, the last looking like a white, visored robot. In the Hudson itself, an ivory and red excursion boat plowed northward. Back on my side of the river, the inland edge of the boulevard had gas stations, Elks and VFWs, and lots of funeral homes. Spaced among them was old-fashioned two-story immigrant housing, upgraded from wood to fieldstone by the second generation. Now it was being disfigured by picture windows and sun decks, courtesy of the yuppies who probably were pushing out the third generation.

"Next stop, buddy."

"Thanks."

Number 6315 was a five-story yellow-brick apartment building on the inland side. Ms. Zerle didn't answer her buzzer any better than she had her phone. I tried the superintendent's button and drew a gut-busting guy wearing a soiled plaid shirt and carrying a can of Piels. When I asked about Ms. Zerle, he waved to a stretch of grass and benches across the street and started to close the door. When I asked him how I'd recognize her, he said, "Can't miss Agnes. She's the only broad wearin' both blue hair and a bikini."

I thanked him and crossed the street.

I guess you could call it a park. There were a few young mothers with kids in strollers, speaking to them and each other in foreign languages or broken English. Mostly, though, there were old people, bundled up even in the warm May sunshine, perhaps three times as many women as men. Next to two young men stretched out on chaise longues was a woman in a tiger-stripe bikini. She looked near seventy, with that leathery surface the elderly get to their skin when they stay in the sun too long. The two men had black, close-cropped hair and a huge boom box radio between them. They were wearing a lot of coconut oil and a little span of Speedo trunks. The woman was tapping one finger against the slack flesh of her right thigh, following the music more than they were.

I said, "Excuse me. Ms. Zerle?"

She opened her eyes, levered up onto an elbow. "Yeah?"

"My name's John Cuddy. I'd like some information about a doctor you might know."

"What makes you think I know him?"

"What makes you think it's a he?"

She rolled back down dismissively. "Because in my time, women weren't what you'd call encouraged to be doctors, so I don't know many that are. And I don't know you, and I'm not interested in answering any questions, so why don't you beat it?"

"Ms. Zerle, I've come a long way on a tough job, and I'd appreciate just a few minutes. I've—"

"Hey, Agnes," said one of the guys, looking first at me, then at her. "You want us to get rid of this guy?"

I was tempted, but I wasn't there to fight. Before she could answer him, I said, "Ms. Zerle, Diana Ross sent me."

The other guy cursed and started to sit up, but Agnes said, "Tony . . ." in a cautionary manner, and he stayed put. She turned to me and said, "Who told you to say that?"

"A guy at the hospital. He handed me this."

She took the paper from me, unfolded and read it. She laughed, offered it back to me. "That's his handwriting, all right. Why don't we move over toward the river. That bench." She said to the first guy, "Sal, watch my stuff, okay?"

He said, "Sure. Yell if you want us."

"Thanks."

Zerle moved toward the bench, me trailing. She strode purposefully, a woman used to walking in order to get from task to task during a busy day. While the unkindness of gravity made everything sag, she still was trim and even graceful in the revealing suit. She sat down, crossed her legs, and said, "Who do you want to know about?"

"A psychiatrist who's working in the Boston area now. I'm helping the defense of a college student. The student is, or rather was, a patient of his who's accused of murdering a girl who was also a patient. There's some indication that the girl and the doctor might have had a relationship outside the therapy group."

"Son, if you'd come to the point, we might finish quicker. You mean sexual relationship?"

"Yes."

"Okay, what's the doctor's name?"

"Marek. Clifford Marek."

She stood up, seemed suddenly chilled. She crossed her arms as Suley had at the hospital, but she shivered a bit and hugged herself.

I started to take off my jacket, but she saw me peripherally and shook her head. "No, no. I'm not cold. It's just . . . Your situation doesn't sound like Marek. No, I don't think so."

"What do you mean?"

"I think you'd better go."

"Look . . ."

"Do you want me to call Sal and Tony over here?"

"No, and I don't want to go a few rounds with them, either. But you're the closest thing to a wedge into this case that I've found, and if that's what it'll take to open you up, then call them."

She sighed, then looked as if she wanted to spit. "Did . . . What's the name of the patient they're accusing?"

"His name is Daniels, William Daniels. He was the dead girl's boyfr—well, lover."

"Daniels."

"Yes."

She took a minute, then made up her mind and asked, face to the river, "This Daniels, is he black?"

TWENTY-SEVEN

"Suley's a female impersonator. On the side, that is, to make a few extra dollars. He does a great Diana Ross. You'd swear you were watching her. More tea?"

I said, "No, thanks," and she looked down into her own cup, wrapping her robe around her more tightly but not speaking. We had come back to her place so that we could talk privately, but she hadn't wanted to get into it, so I was smart for a change and didn't push.

"Yeah, old Suley—and he is old, don't let that unlined face and swishy style fool you; Suley, he's pushing forty-five—old Suley is a talented fella, and a smart one too. He would have had my job when I retired if he just weren't such a flamer that he made everybody upstairs nervous. So instead they bring in Smith from some small law firm she was running—as office manager; she's not a lawyer herself—and old Suley stays where he is."

Zerle played with her spoon, started to wring out a little more from the tea bag into her cup, then put everything down. She said, "If I talk to you now, what are the chances of me having to testify about it?"

"In court in Boston?"

"Yeah."

"I could be cute and say I won't know that until I've heard what you've got to say, but basically I don't know. I'm not a lawyer, either. But I think you ought to assume you might have to. This is a murder case, and I think that witnesses can be made to cross state lines if they have important enough information. It might be out of my hands."

Zerle seemed to like honest better than cute. She sank back into her chair and started speaking, slowly, as though she were narrating for children.

"It happened in the early seventies sometime. The records would have the exact dates and all, if the records are still there, and they were there when I left four years ago. Marek came to us as a psychiatry resident. He was on a two-year program. I think he didn't go right to medical school from college, because he seemed older somehow than the other residents, but I'm not too sure now. Anyway, he came in, and was assigned some groups, and individuals, and began treating them. It was a while before anything . . . before anybody started saying anything, but there was something not quite right about him. Like he'd have the most interest in some of the easiest cases and spend too much time on them and not enough on some of the real bad ones he had. Usually, that just means the chief resident or even somebody higher has a talk with him, and he straightens out his priorities. But with Marek, I don't know, it didn't seem so much like oversight on his part as intention, that he started to sneak the time to see these less sick patients. What was weird is that he was doing all right by his other patients—the real bad ones, I mean. He was doing average anyway, if you're talking in terms of results. But anyone who dealt with him could tell he really had a knack of cutting through and getting to most of the sick ones, and so we kind of resented, I guess, his not spending the time with them so that his knack could work more good for them. Then some of the patients . . .'' She looked up at me.

"Yes?"

She looked down again. ''The black patients, they started saying things, at first among themselves, then some of the braver ones to us—to me, that is. That Marek was, well, using them for sex. At first, you tend to dismiss that kind of talk. I mean, you really can't take straight what most of the patients say because a lot of them are in there because of what they say. But the talk, not complaints so much as just gossip, started to get out of hand and then one of them . . .'' She stopped, but this time she didn't look to me for a prompt, so I kept still.

Zerle made a noise with her tongue off the roof of her mouth. ''One of the patients got a cord off some blinds somewhere and hanged himself. He left kind of a note, about Marek. That tore it. I thought, if only I'd done something sooner. But the dead patient was black, destitute, and had no family we knew of, so nothing happened directly to the hospital. We had an internal review, and Marek left soon after that.''

She didn't appear to be close to starting again, so I said, ''I had the impression that when Marek came to Massachusetts, part of the application was a certification from his last job and state, in Illinois, that he was basically competent and of good character.''

"Probably."

"But how?"

"How?"

"How could he go from here even to Philly, which was his next stop, much less on to Chicago and then Boston, with this kind of a mess in his record?"

A faint smile of experience faded quickly. "We didn't fire him, Mr. Cuddy. We allowed him to resign from the hospital's residency program.''

"Why?"

"Because of what he did."

"Yes, but why was he allowed to resign? Why didn't you fire him?"

"I would have. But it wasn't my decision to make, though I understood the necessity for it at the time.''

"Can you explain it to me?"

"I can try." She hunched forward, punctuating with her hands. "Let's say you run a hospital, okay? You've got lots of bills for lots of things, most of all new equipment. But you don't really have enough money, not nearly enough, because the care costs more than we charge for it, and we don't get even as much as we charge because of deadbeats or insurance companies short-sheeting us on reimbursements. Every department feels it's understaffed, underpaid, and underappreciated. And every department is right. So you're in charge, and a question comes up about this guy Marek, and you sit down with him and probably his lawyer, and the situation stacks up like this: Marek is willing to resign quietly, which cuts the hospital loose of a bad doc. The alternative for you is to fire Marek for what he did, both with the dead patient and with the others, and to report Marek to every certifying board in sight. Now, you do that, and it's curtains for Marek as any kind of doctor in this country, so he's got to fight it, and I mean to the end, with everything he's got. And maybe one thing he's got is some shady things that other people in the hospital have done, maybe things that were done to help the patients, but maybe some cooking of reimbursement requests or vouchers, or drug supplies, or anything that the media would jump on. So there you are. You're in charge. What are your options?''

"Let him resign quietly or fire him and spend your overextended dollars on legal fees as he fights for his professional life?''

"You've got it. So which do you do?''

"I don't know. One way you protect your institution, but at the expense of health care generally. I don't know.''

"Add in something else. Add in that you might lose.''

"Lose?''

"Yeah. As in lose the fight. Maybe Marek fights and wins.''

"But you said—''

"That a bunch of fruity patients said he was doing all kinds of things to them that a good doctor shouldn't. You ever met Marek?''

"Yes.''

"Impressive as hell, isn't he?''

"Yes.''

"You're on a jury. A postal worker, or maybe a housewife. You listen to the three or four black wackos presentable enough to put on a witness stand tell their side of it, then you watch some high-powered attorney that Marek's hired rip the stuffing out of their stories. Then you see Marek himself up there. Calm, educated, persuasive. Embarrassed but forthright about these ridiculous claims. He tells the jurors not to judge his accusers too harshly. Who're you gonna believe? Moses incarnate, or some nutcakes just a trifle softer than Suley?''

I thought about it. I didn't think the hospital had been morally right, but it was hard to second-guess the decision as a business judgment.

I said, "About Suley . . . ?"

She grew guarded. "Yeah?"

"When he gave me your name, he knew only that I was interested in Marek, not anything about a black patient being involved."

"So?"

"So why would he have wanted to help me?"

"He was on the job maybe six months when Marek arrived. Some of us thought it was Suley who nudged the patients to come talk to me. Marek . . . I think Suley just thought Marek was a dishonorable man."

When I finished with Agnes Zerle, we walked out to the boulevard. She pointed to a three-sided glass enclosure with a white bubble top and the New Jersey Transit logo on it. "You can catch the 165 back into Port Authority there. Funny, they used to call the company 'Public Service' in the old days. Now it's 'New Jersey Transit.' Sign of the times, I guess."

I thanked her again, and we shook hands. She walked back toward the apartment building, robe flapping around her legs and the determination gone from her stride.

I got into Port Authority about 4:30 P.M. After grabbing a quick bite at a workingman's tavern on Eighth Avenue, I walked the rest of the way to Penn Station. I retrieved my bag from its locker and just made the next train to Boston.

It was a long ride, nearly five hours. But I needed the

time to think. To rethink, actually. We clacked along the Connecticut coast, past the clubbiness of Stamford and the grubbiness of Bridgeport, the last sailboats of the evening slipping gracefully into Old Saybrook harbor. I took apart and reworked everything I knew, this time with William, not Jennifer, as Marek's centerpiece. What must have happened. And what I was going to be able to do about it.

TWENTY-EIGHT

A night of sleeping in my own bed did me a world of good. Looking back on the events of the next twenty-four hours, however, I made three bad mistakes. One was calling Steve Rothenberg, finding out that he would be on trial in another matter all day, and deciding that I didn't need to speak with him. The second mistake was calling Lieutenant Murphy, finding out he was unavailable too, and deciding that I didn't really need him, either. The third will become pretty obvious.

The phone call I did complete appeared successful at the time. O'Boy set up the meeting I wanted in Calem, and the young assistant prosecutor there seemed cooperative. He also seemed pretty chummy with Chief Wooten, but I just assumed they had worked together before.

I was in front of Marek's office building before 5:00 P.M. I took the stairs and entered his reception area just as Mrs. Porter was gathering her things and closing up shop. She looked up, recognized me this time, and scowled.

"Is he in?" I said.

"Dr. Marek is very busy. He's preparing a paper and cannot—"

I started walking toward his inner door.

She said, "Wait, you can't just . . . Dr. Marek, Dr. Marek!"

I got to the door and opened it as Marek was rising behind his desk. He was in shirtsleeves, with a portable computer humming in front of him.

"What do you want?" he said, clipping off each word.

The receptionist behind me said, "He just pushed his way in, Doctor. I . . ."

Marek said, "It's all right, Mrs. Porter. I'm sure it wasn't your fault." Then, to me: "Mr. Cuddy, we've concluded our business together. I would appreciate your leaving. Now."

"I think you ought to hear me out on this one, Doc."

"Now."

"I really do."

"Mrs. Porter, please call the police, and tell—"

"You see, it's about Agnes Zerle, and Jerome Gemelman, and . . ."

I stopped, because Marek's face had gone from ruddy to ashen. He said, "Mrs. Porter, I'm sorry. I do have to speak with Mr. Cuddy. You may leave for the day."

"But, Dr. Marek . . ."

"No, no," he said, his soothing voice back on track. "It's all right. I know what Mr. Cuddy wants to talk about, and the police won't be necessary. Thank you, though."

She looked apprehensively at Marek, then combatively

at me before she left the room, closing the door behind her.

"Take a seat," he said as he punched some buttons on the computer and then turned some dials on his other console. As the computer drone died, Marek frowned and adjusted the dials some more before he sat back down.

He said, "It's rather warm in here, which is how I like it when I'm writing. Would you care to take your jacket off?"

Marek was right about the temperature, but I said, "No, thanks."

He rested his elbows on the desk surface and tented his fingers in front of his chin. "Now, why do you want to talk with me about dear Ms. Zerle?"

"I think you already know."

"Why assume that?"

"Because of what she could have told me."

"Ah, Mr. Cuddy, am I now to make some sort of slip that you'll use to nab me under whatever absurd theory you're pursuing?"

"Nab you for what?"

"Sir, you keep dangling the worm, and I keep ignoring the bait. Why don't you simply tell me what you want so that both of us can progress to more productive endeavors?"

"Fine, Doctor. You killed Jennifer Creasey. You also killed Lainie Bishop to cover it."

Marek laughed and rocked back into his chair. "This sounds like quite a thorough delusion on your part, Mr. Cuddy. Perhaps I should take the time to hear you out. For professional curiosity, I mean."

"I have to give you credit, Doctor. At least for Jennifer. The way I see it, you must have had to act quickly and under considerable pressure."

"Please go on."

"You're comfortably established in a fine community like Calem. You channel an underside to your personality to keep that community from discovering the truth. You do competent, maybe even brilliant work . . ."

"Why, thank you."

" . . . but then you get a little careless. You have this group that you'd like to expand. You were happy to have Jennifer come to you. Her family connections could lead to more rich new clients. She was obviously attracted to you, but you must have learned how to deal with flirtatious female patients a long time ago. You just kept your professional demeanor with her, a fiduciary who wouldn't think of trading on a relationship for sexual satisfaction. However, you still wanted a more diverse group for your experiment, and lo and behold, Jennifer brings you a dilemma. William Daniels. Ghetto to greatness. Young, bright, and good-looking to boot. Slim, taut-muscled, features like a male model."

"Perhaps," said Marek, clearing his throat, "if you could get to the point."

"I'd love to, Doctor, but it's a complicated story, and I don't want you to feel I've missed any of it. Anyway, Jennifer offers William to you—for the group, that is—and you can't even make an argument against him. He's exactly the right person to round out the experiment. So you accept him, probably figuring you can control it. Keep the patient from becoming a target, I mean."

Marek just looked at me.

"I'm guessing the first time you really didn't try to arrange it. Probably William came to you, maybe just early on one of the group's Thursdays. He poured out his soul to you, all the problems he'd been having, with Jennifer, grades, the shits who were harassing him at school. Was there something about him, his body language, maybe? Whatever, something broke the camel's back. First you told him you were going to relax him with an injection of flurazepam. Then you hypnotized him, told him he should ignore any discomfort he might feel afterwards. And then you did him.''

Marek's eyes were ablaze, his lips tight. ''Nonsense.''

''And he was good, maybe great. The anxiety, the torment, all the energy that builds up from those emotions, it all came rushing out, and you knew this was too good to pass up in the future. So you handled the transition from the trance in a way that ensured he consciously remembered nothing. And the next time, William just shows up a little early again. To start, probably only on his Thursdays, the ones when he's going to be the subject of the group session. I bet you got a bit of a jolt the first time you found the gun on him, but I'm sure that you could understand his explanation for it, that the other kids back home in Roxbury might need strong persuading to leave their upwardly mobile neighbor alone. Maybe the revolver even heightened things a bit for you. The street kid on the rise, Goreham with a dash of gun oil? Great thrill, precious little risk, and even that minimized. After all, you're his psychiatrist, right? The person he'd come to if anything started to surface. You know what I mean?''

''Of course not.''

''Oh, come on now, Doctor. Surely William told you about the nightmares.''

No response.

''You remember. The visions of what you made him do. The visions that you blocked off from his conscious mind by the hypnosis. They'd have to surface somewhere, sometime. Professor Kirby—he's at BU—we had a nice chat about all this—''

229

Marek came forward as if someone had kicked the back of his chair. "How dare you . . ."

"Oh, all in the hypothetical, of course. He and I just talked about how a suppressed memory like that would come up when the suppression state—here, wakefulness—was supplanted by sleep. That was really good of you, Doc, you know? Taking away from the kid the peace of sleep, the one time that he could forget about the things that were driving him crazy."

"This is all rubbish. You have no proof whatever for any of this."

"Bear with me, Doctor, bear with me. You covered your trail pretty well, but you couldn't know about William's tapes unless—"

Marek said, "What t—" then caught himself.

"His audiotapes. William recorded his nightmares. Interesting stuff on those tapes. But there was other evidence of what you were doing to William. Jennifer confided in some people. She let on that William the Stud was declining somewhat in his performance. Not surprising, what with you tuckering him out on Thursdays early evening, when Thursdays after group were probably their most likely times to get together. My guess is she wondered why, though. Do you suppose she noticed that William was always here before everybody else on Thursdays? Or did she just figure that if she came to you well before group and told you about William's problem, the sexual-function talk might just turn you on? Jennifer was a girl who liked to experiment herself, a girl who was used to getting whatever, or whomever, she went after. Jennifer came up here early that Thursday night, didn't she, Doctor?"

"I don't know what—"

"She rode the elevator up, walked through the front

door, and came to your inner-office door to knock. But maybe she listened at the door first. And heard funny sounds she recognized. She came in on you. She started laughing, calling you names; maybe both. Your past flashed through your mind—New York, Philly, Chicago— but those were just brushes with the authorities. Getting away with punching street kids was one thing. William, now, he was the lover of a headstrong girl from a powerful family, a girl who knew how to dish it out to lovers, especially older lovers, who rejected her. She knew how to get you. My guess is that you remembered William's gun, that she was laughing at you even while you tried to pull up your pants and rummage for wherever you kept it when William was here. Then Jennifer saw the gun and probably the look on your face. She bolted out the door, instinctively down the stairs instead of risking a wait for the elevator. A little late for the dentists and all, and a little early for the group's other members to be drifting in. You chased her down the stairs. That must have been quite a sight, huh, Doc?"

Marek ground his teeth.

"Anyway, she's used to taking the elevator, not the stairs, so as she's flying down she misses the lobby level and realizes too late that she's hit the bottom, the basement. She panics and heads through the only door that opens, the one to the boiler room. You corner her in there. She turns on you, tries to tough it out with threats. Or does she start making fun of you again, of what you are?"

Marek closed his eyes.

"Maybe you didn't mean to kill her. Maybe you didn't even realize the gun was going off. But suddenly you did, maybe after the second shot, maybe after the third. But in any case, there she was. Fortunately, you hadn't emptied the gun into her. But what to do? And not much time to do it in. Then you remembered William. Tell me, Marek, when you got back upstairs, was William still in the same position? Was he still waiting for you? As though you had just gotten up to change a phonograph record instead of having killed the girl he clearly if stupidly loved?''

"What would you know about it?"

His eyes were still closed, but it was a crack in the facade. I hoped there'd be more. "So you get back to William, and tell him to get dressed. You take him down to the boiler room, hand him the gun you've already wiped off. You tell him to fire at the wall, or maybe you tell him some bad guys, like the kids in the neighborhood, are armed and coming at him, tell him to kill them before they kill him. Either way, William fires, then you tell him to put the gun in his pocket, then you tell him he's just shot Jennifer. You ask him how he could have done such a thing. He gets agitated, terribly upset. You tell him there's only one way for him ever to feel better again, and that's to tell the group about shooting her, that once he does that he'll be able to forget everything else that happened. All the pain, all the horror, all gone once he tells the group and shows them the gun. You tell him to wait down there, maybe for a while, maybe till a certain time. Then you leave him there, in the basement, staring at Jennifer's body and breaking apart inside."

"I think," said Marek in a tired voice, "that this has gone far enough, even for a delusion."

"Unfortunately for William, it hasn't. That night you came back up here and waited for the other members of the group. As they arrived, you welcomed them as though nothing had happened, as though the only annoyance in the world was the thoughtless tardiness of Jennifer and William. Then, however, you realized something. You'd had William shoot at the wall so that when his hands were tested by the cops they'd find evidence that he had recently fired a gun. But they'd also test him for drugs, and that would mean both chemically and visibly, like looking at his arms for needle marks. That presented a problem, didn't it? You'd already injected him once, before playtime. If you gave him another shot, during the session, there'd be two needle marks on his arm and too much drug in his system. So you asked Lainie to move, to change her chair, so that you could palm or fake the session injection of William.''

Marek suddenly looked almost relieved. ''Cuddy, this is ridiculous. If I had done even remotely as you suggest, then over the weeks that I was 'preying' on poor William I would have to have been 'palming' his session dosage. And that just doesn't hold up. The late Lainie would have seen me from her chair, and I never asked anyone, Lainie or anyone else, to move any other night.''

''So Homer told me. And that bothered me a lot. I could understand your slipping up that night under the pressure of Jennifer's murder, but what about all the other sessions?''

''Precisely.''

''But then I figured out what must have happened the previous Thursdays. If I'm right, you had a choice those other nights. First, give no drug at all in the session, palming the syringe every night. As you said, the problem with that is that you would have been seen, by a member or by the videotape. A second choice would be to give William a placebo, like a harmless injection of sugar water. That would leave two fresh needle marks instead of one, but as long as William wasn't going to be examined those other nights, no problem. Also, with the placebo approach you wouldn't have to palm the needle, for Lainie and all to spot.''

Marek nearly smiled. "Yes, but if I had a placebo ready for that night's session already, and if I were worried about how much flurazepam a postsession blood test would detect, I simply would have given William the placebo that night, as well."

"That's right."

Now Marek did smile, in his patronizing way. "And therefore, I—"

"—never did use a placebo. In those earlier sessions, I mean."

Marek stopped smiling. "But you said either . . ."

"No, I said you had choices, palming or placebo. But in fact you had a third choice at the earlier group sessions, the choice you actually made."

"Really. What?"

"Give William another shot of flurazepam."

"Why on earth would I do that?"

"At first, when you began your private sessions with William, you must have used a greater than normal dose of flurazepam anyway to 'relax' him. According to Professor Kirby, flurazepam really isn't an anxiolytic, a tranquilizer. It's more a true hypnotic, meaning a sleeping potion. Even very diluted, it would still be stronger than most true tranquilizers. Kirby says that while it would take some time to build up a tolerance to flurazepam, increased usage would do it. I'm betting that over the months you had to give William an increasing amount of flurazepam before your times with him, in order to hypnotize him into doing, and letting you do, certain things. So, at the earlier group sessions, it was probably safer just to give him another shot of the stuff, to make sure he was still under."

"Not acceptable, Cuddy. I begin every group session by asking the subject where he or she has been during the preceding hour. Clearly, if I'd been sodomizing William he would have revealed that.''

I shook my head. "Not necessarily. You could have blocked that memory from surfacing at the group sessions by sufficient flurazepam earlier and a posthypnotic suggestion implanted in William before you turned him loose.''

"And what, pray tell, are your credentials in pharmacology and hypnosis?''

"Slim to none. But Kirby's are impeccable, and I have a feeling he'll back me on that possibility.''

"Still rubbish. Why, then, would I not just inject William in group that night too?''

"With more flurazepam, you mean?''

"Yes,'' he said, testily.

"That closes the circle. Like I said, you realized at some point after you killed Jennifer that the police would examine William both chemically and visibly. For what it's worth, they did. But when they looked at his arm, you wanted them to see only one fresh track mark. And you also were probably afraid that another shot, at the group session now, of flurazepam would show up as off the scale in any blood test. That would be difficult for you to explain. Homer, and I expect Ramelli too, would say William seemed lethargic at group many nights. How could you get the police to buy that a group member like William who appeared lethargic to start with had somehow been built up over the course of your care to tolerating enough flurazepam to cool a killer whale? No, you faced a real predicament, Doctor. Shoot William again with flurazepam and run those risks, or ask Lainie to move so you could fake it.''

"Sheer conjecture.''

"But Lainie fooled you, didn't she? She wouldn't move.

Tell me, Marek, did you realize then that you'd be having more trouble with her?''

He sat impassive now, a Buddha statue in a handsome Caucasian body. "I don't know what you mean."

"Sure you do. Jennifer confided in Lainie, thought Lainie had the world—probably meaning men and sex—all figured out. I saw Lainie in action at a bar. She seemed a good listener for people in trouble. Maybe Jennifer confided that she was going to see you earlier that Thursday, maybe Lainie was just being coy to attract you herself. Whichever, Lainie didn't move, and you had to try to cover yourself anyway. You remembered to dim and up the lights but not to turn on the video equipment. . . ."

"I told you. I told the police. I was rattled by William's—"

"No sale, Doc. You're a trained professional, used to dealing with agitated people. If anything, William's state should have triggered your videotaping him, not squelched it. No, you failed to start the camera so no record would exist of your palming the needle. Then you botched your act, and Lainie spotted it. Is that why she was the one who went down to the basement with you to check on William's story? Did Lainie confront you there? Or was it later? Was Lainie still interested in you romantically?"

"You are crazy," a slight rise in Marek's voice, clipping off his words again.

"My guess is she was more than interested in you. My guess is Lainie had fallen for you, truly, and didn't know quite how to show that, the real thing. Or maybe it was just business as usual for her. She tried to hit me up to tell her about any divorce cases I was working on. Lainie worked the angles, and she wanted a little advance notice if a couple might be needing to put their house on the market, maybe with an aggressive, effective sales broker like her to push it. I've given it a lot of thought, Marek, and I'm betting either she was really in love with you or she tried to blackmail you, maybe for straight money, maybe for names of patients who were in the kind of trouble where their homes might have to be sold."

"Lainie Bishop was a slut, Mr. Cuddy. Pure and simple. When her ex-husband realized it, he bailed out. I think you're giving the dear departed Ms. Bishop too much credit for brains."

"But you didn't, did you? You knew just how gullible she might be with the right kind of encouragement. You made it sound to her like you might enjoy supplying her with more than money or names. You arranged a little rendezvous with her at her house. Then you killed her and made it look like the town burglar had panicked. Exit the Cheshire cat from another potentially embarrassing professional snafu."

"You're mad, Cuddy. Clinically and literally. Mad."

"I don't think so. I think the way I described it is about what happened."

Marek made a noise deep in his chest, like a mountain about to slough off in avalanche a couple hundred tons of ice and snow. He leaned forward again. "You ever kill anyone, Cuddy?"

I thought for a second. "Not that we can talk about."

He started to laugh, then choked a little. "After what you've just put me through, 'Not that we can . . . ' Well, let me tell you, my friend, you have no idea what hell is until . . . How do you think I felt about Lester Briles, that boy at New York Central? How do you think it feels to be pushed to do something that every part of you but one says will be wonderful, and the one part says is despicable?"

"If the one part's your conscience, I'd say it ought to feel pretty human."

237

"Don't patronize me!" he snapped, slamming his hand flat on the desktop. "I've had enough of your 'homo' innuendoes. You despise me, don't you? You despise me because I go down on black boys and bugger them."

"No, Marek. I despise you, all right, but not for being gay. I despise you because of the way you traded on a relationship. You took advantage of people, of patients, who were coming to you professionally for treatment."

"Mr. High and Might—"

"A professional's supposed to be like the keeper in a game preserve. Only you fed the animals out of your hand one day and gunned them down the next. You killed two innocent, at least relatively innocent, people and did your best to ruin a third, all of them in your care. That's what I despise."

Marek snorted. "So what do you do now, detective? Do you kill *me?*"

"I thought about it. After I figured out what you did, I thought about it."

Marek's eyes opened wider. He started to speak, then stopped.

I said, "But then I decided it wouldn't do any good."

Marek recovered. "Why not? People with delusions like yours often believe that revenge is its own reward."

"Maybe. But only when it also solves the problem. Killing you might square your crimes, but I'd go to jail, and William wouldn't necessarily get out."

"I see," said Marek ponderously. "So you want me to turn myself in. To make the grand gesture of self-confession to free what you see as my wrongly accused patient."

"No, just the opposite. I want you to run."

Marek stared at me. He finally said, "You want me to what?"

"Run. Soon, like tomorrow, maybe. And far, as far as you can."

"Why in God's name would I do that?"

"Because either way, you're finished here. And as a psychiatrist, anywhere."

"I don't follow you."

"Okay, I'll go slowly. Let's say you stonewall it and try to stay in Calem. You and I both know what actually happened. I go to the cops, they investigate a little deeper. They look at the records in New York and other places. They bring in Zerle, maybe Gemelman too. They go back to Lainie's, find some piece of physical evidence like threads from a coat to tie you there. They have a superstar hypnotist deprogram William, unravel those mistaken recollections you planted in his head."

"None of this would begin to stand up in court."

"It wouldn't have to. I'd just have to smear you enough that your professional life in this area would be a memory. A bad memory that would stick in people's minds."

"Then why should I run, if you'll ruin me anyway?"

"Because if you don't run, there's at least a chance that things will stand up in court, and you'll be nailed, civilly and criminally. If you stay, you're ruined and maybe jailed. If you run, you're ruined but free. Free to be anything you want to be. Except, of course, a psychiatrist or doctor again."

"What makes you so sure of that?"

"The licensing procedure. Every state has one of some kind. I'll see to it that you never get licensed again anywhere, even if you stay and beat the killings. The reason you've been able to hop from state to state like a migrating predator is that each hospital you were leaving had too much to lose in really dealing with you. I don't have anything to lose. I'll just hound you. Forever."

Marek puffed up his lower lip. "But if I run, I get away with it. If you're right—that is, if I killed Jennifer and Lainie—you'd be letting me get away with murder."

"Not my job."

"What?"

"It's not my job to see you get convicted. My worry is getting William off. If you run, combined with the story I give the cops about you, my guess is the DA either dismisses the indictment or runs a serious risk of losing a trial on the reasonable-doubt question. He wouldn't want the resultant embarrassing publicity as everyone realizes he'd tried the wrong man and no one knows where you are."

"Whereas if I stay, I'm still around to deny things."

"Right, but you're also around to be nailed yourself."

A full minute wound by before Marek spoke again. "Why don't you just get out of here?"

I stood up. "Sure. Just don't take too long to think it over. And when you make up your mind to run, don't even call me. Just disappear. And wonder what god you should thank for sparing you again."

I backed out of the room and closed the door. I crossed the waiting area and was out that door too. I rode the elevator down. Outside, I started my car and drove around the corner. I stopped behind a nondescript panel truck parked near a telephone pole. As I got out of my car, Chief Wooten came through the back doors of the van.

"I think he'll run," I said, unbuttoning my shirt and reaching in for the tape holding the transmitter under my right nipple.

"We didn't get all of it," said Wooten, crossing his arms so that the Navy tattoo was facing me.

"What?" I said, tearing the transmitter free and drawing it out. I even forgot to rub the burning, tender spot the tape left.

O'Boy stuck his head out the doors, a pair of earphones down around his neck like a high-tech slave collar. "We got bits and pieces, Cuddy. We heard you and the receptionist fine, and Marek telling you to take a seat. But after that, static, bird noises, and maybe every other sentence. Granted I'm no expert on this stuff, but it was like we were being jammed or something."

I closed my eyes. Marek had a lot of electronic equipment in that office, and he fiddled with the dials on that control panel the last two times I'd talked with him. When he thought I could be coming after him. Dammit.

Wooten said, "Cuddy, with what we did get, it sounded to me like he admitted it. Killing both the girl and the Bishop woman."

I looked at him. "Yes, but never in so many words."

"The hell's that supposed to mean?"

"It's supposed to mean that he outfoxed me, Chief. He spotted the wire. Electronically. He confirmed it when I passed up taking off my coat in a hot room. He knew all the time I was trying to trap him, and he interfered with the signal back to the truck."

"So?"

"So he was playing me when I thought I was playing him, Chief. Get it now? He was just using me to find out what I had on him. Now he knows. And by spotting the wire, he knows you suspect him too."

O'Boy said, "Not necessarily."

I looked at O'Boy, who continued talking. "Lots of private outfits have this kind of gear now. He might have known you were wired, but still not be sure you're working with us."

O'Boy had a point. I said, "Then what do you think we should do?"

O'Boy said, "You went through his alternatives with him, right? I mean, we heard parts of the run/don't run, and all that shit."

"Yes."

"Then I say we wait him out. Two, three days, anyway. Maybe he still sees the sense of it, that both Daniels and him are better off if he runs. Then we grab him on the fly."

Wooten waved his arm like a semaphore and said, "I say we take the faggot now."

I started, "Chief—"

"No," spat Wooten. "You and him talked, Cuddy. Christ, he admitted queering the boy and killing the two females. What more do you think you're gonna get?"

"Chief," said O'Boy. "Please wait a minute."

"No, I've waited long enough on this case. The papers, Creasey's fucking TV station, the whole world's gonna wonder what the hell took so long to figure out anyway. If we don't take him now, there's a dozen ways we could lose him." A Calem PD cruiser screeched to a halt beside Wooten, and he opened the passenger side to get in.

I talked as fast as I could. "Chief, even if the guy had admitted everything to me chapter and verse, without a complete tape of it the DA's got only my word against Marek's, and I'm impeachable as hell because of my interest in helping Daniels get off."

"No."

I started to suggest that he at least wait to consult the young prosecutor that we'd worked it out with that afternoon, but you can't argue with taillights. As Wooten sped off toward Marek's building, I looked at O'Boy. He shrugged and disappeared back into the van.

TWENTY-NINE

◆

The clock in the bedroom said only 6:30 A.M., but I wanted to arrive at Middlesex early enough to see William privately before Marek's arraignment. I had reached Mrs. Daniels by telephone the night before, and she thanked me profusely through her tears. I wanted her to be the first to tell William the good news. I left only a blind "call me" message for Rothenberg with his answering service. I left the same for Murphy with Detective Cross, who said that the lieutenant would probably be gone for the night on a possible murder/suicide in Bay Village.

I was knotting my tie when the telephone rang. I picked it up. "Hello?"

"Cuddy. I got a message from Cross that you called me last night."

"That's right."

"Cross said Willa called too. I thought maybe I'd better

talk with you first. What's up?" He barely spoke the last part, sounding dead tired.

"The Calem cops arrested Marek yesterday for Jennifer Creasey's murder. It looks like William's going to be clear of it."

Murphy's voice revived. "No shit?"

"Straight. They're arraigning Marek this morning."

"That's awful quick to . . . Damn, I haven't gotten any sleep with this murder/suicide thing. . . ."

"Cross told me. Why don't I call you later today with the details on Marek?"

"Yeah. Yeah, that'd be good." He stopped. "I don't mean to put you off, Cuddy. I really appreciate your dogging this one."

"Glad to do it." While William could probably use a father figure about now, I decided that for once I'd like to part with Murphy cordially. The suggestion could wait too. "Get some sleep."

"Right. Hear from you later."

I hung up and finished dressing.

I got to the courthouse building so early I walked in with the camera crew from Channel 8, the TV station covering the courts that morning. As a woman in the Middlesex County Police security team checked me through the metal detector in the lobby, a man in the team joked with a cameraman.

"Christ, Manny," said the officer, glancing into one of the big black cases the cameraman was hauling. "Think you got enough videotape there?"

"Tell my hernia about it," said Manny. "The boss, Creasey himself, wanted it all brought in, all the tape of the Daniels kid plus the blanks for today."

"Why, for chrissakes?"

"Creasey's a nut for some things, you know? He wants

us to line up the camera today on this shrink guy exactly, and I mean exactly, the way we had it on Daniels.''

"Spooky."

"Yeah. I figure maybe it's 'cause this'll be his last go-round."

"I don't get you."

"Didn't you hear? Fucking FCC yanked our license yesterday."

"No! You mean you're off the air?"

"Not right away. There's court stuff they gotta go through and all. But the way people were talking at the station last night, it don't look good."

"Gee, Manny, I'm sorry."

"Yeah. Gotta give the boss credit, though. He gets hit with that yesterday, but still checks us out this morning before we leave the station. Goes through every fucking tape himself while we're getting the rest of our stuff, making sure we didn't miss one. Not just the arraignment, either. The arrest, the witnesses coming in and out of the building here. The works. Some people, y'know?"

The crew and I caught the same elevator. They got off at the ninth floor while I continued to the seventeenth, trying to push Sam Creasey's problems out of my mind.

William's first words to me were "The fuck do you want?"

I guess I didn't expect a bear hug, but I said, "I called your mother last night. Didn't she get the word to you about Marek?"

"Yeah. She made like you figured that he was punking me."

"Basically."

"Great fucking news."

"But, William, it means—"

"It means—" he shouted, then he lowered his voice to a raspy but conversational level. "It means that I did things with him and to him and it's gonna be all over the news tonight."

"Yes, but it also means you're off the hook for Jennifer's murder. You didn't kill her, and the police and everybody know you didn't."

"Yeah, terrific. But the police and everybody don't got to do a year with the wrong kind of sign hanging around their necks, you dig?"

"What do you mean . . . ?"

"Jail, man. In-car-cer-a-tion. Twelve fucking months for the gun charge. Or did you forget about that?"

"I guess I did."

"Yeah, well, too bad you ain't running the system. They ain't gonna forget about it."

"Maybe Rothenberg can work something out."

William shook his head. "You don't know shit, man. Gun charge is automatic. No deals, no probation, no parole. One year gone."

"Look, they've got to control for things, at least. They'll give you credit for the time you've already served."

"Oh, great, man! Wonderful system. One down, just eleven to go, huh?" He hitched his seat forward, clenching and unclenching his fists and his teeth. "Well, let me tell you something, mother'. This the same system that encourage me to step up in class. To go from home to U Mass, and U Mass to Goreham. But it didn't 'control' for the bloods back on Millrose Street that made me buy the piece, or the dudes in the dorm at Goreham, or the shrink who was supposed to be helping me instead of helping himself *to* me. You got that, Jack? This system of yours has fucked me but good. And now it's gonna keep on fucking me by way of any mother' doing hard time with a hard on. Thanks, man. Thanks a lot for all you and your system done for me."

William stood and gestured impatiently for the guard.

The proceedings against Marek were to be held in courtroom 9A. Like most of the new courthouse, 9A was carpeted and acoustically perfect, a modern butcher-block arena for deciding which side had hired the better lawyer.

The camera crew was still setting up off to the left. The courtroom was nearly half full already, and it looked like old home week. I could see Chief Wooten talking intently with a shrugging guy at the district attorney's table. Officers Clay and Bjorkman were sitting in the first row. When Clay saw me, he got up and said something to the chief. The prosecutor looked at me and mouthed "Him?" Clay nodded and the prosecutor, now ignoring Wooten, started walking back toward me. Before he reached me, I spotted Homer Linden in one corner on the left waving to me sociably and the backs of Sam and Tyne Creasey in the first row on the right. Sam Creasey stood and moved over to his camera crew, directing one of them. Then Creasey began looking through one of the big black cases as the prosecutor drew even with me and said, "C'mon."

"You're kidding."

He said, "Wish I was."

The assistant district attorney's name was Gibson. He was sturdy and paramilitary in a three-piece suit. I didn't like what I'd just heard him tell me in the little conference room outside 9A.

"You mean that even if the tape had come out perfectly, it still wouldn't be admissible?"

"That's right. You want the short version or the long one?"

"The short one, please."

"Okay. We have a statute in this commonwealth, call it Section Ninety-nine. That statue says generally that the police can't tape a conversation without a warrant. Section Ninety-nine has an exception, though, that basically says that if one party to a conversation agrees to the interception, then we don't need the others to consent nor do we need a warrant."

"That's what happened, though. I was a party to the conversation, and I agreed to the taping."

"Yeah, but the exception requires you to be a law enforcement officer, which, even stretching things, you aren't. And the taping has to be done to prove certain 'designated offenses' connected to some kind of 'organized crime.' Our boy Marek doesn't fit."

"So what does that mean? Aside from the fact we can't use the tape."

Gibson tugged on an earlobe. "It means that you, Wooten, and O'Boy broke the law."

I stood up, walked over to the window to calm down. "The assistant DA yesterday, the one Wooten and O'Boy and I met with before the taping. He approved all this."

"That kid's been in the office barely a year. Wooten calls him—he's Wooten's brother-in-law's kid, by the way—Wooten calls him with this maybe big case opportunity, so the kid speed-reads the statute, Section Ninety-nine. The kid misses the organized-crime part, which is interpreted in Supreme Judicial Court cases and elaborated in a *Massachusetts Law Review* article to the point where a dim ten-year-old could deal with it. The kid, however, misses it, like I said, signs out the wire equipment, and . . . Well, you know the rest."

I turned back to Gibson. "Does this foul-up mean that even I can't testify on what Marek told me?"

"Hard to say. The statute just limits recording or eavesdropping on conversations. A party to the conversation should still be able to testify about what the prospective defendant, here Marek, said during the conversation."

I thought about it. Even embellished, my version of what was said wouldn't be convincing. "If you were to handicap it right now, what would you say?"

"Too early to tell."

"Meaning I've got a great theory, we both believe Marek's the killer, but you don't have the ammunition to prove it."

"Like I said, it's too early. Hell, we're months from the trial, and evidence has a way of falling into your lap. I'll tell you this, though. Marek's hired himself one of the best. If there's a rug this can be swept under for him, the lawyer you'll see today is the broom that can do it." He stood up. "We'd better be getting back in."

Gibson moved up the aisle. There was a new face at the otherwise empty defense table. A distinguished, graying man who shook hands with and smiled at Gibson. A lawyerly replica of Marek. I felt sick.

"John?"

I turned my head. It was Sam Creasey. He had one of those black, snap-open videocassette cases in one hand and a concerned look on his face. "Sam, I heard about the license. I'm—"

"That can wait. I saw you go out with the prosecutor. What's going on?"

I shook my head. "Nothing, Sam. He just wanted to hear my side of it."

"John, please don't bullshit me on this. It's too important. What is it?"

I tried looking him in the eye, but it wasn't easy. "The

prosecutor didn't say it this bluntly, but I don't think he can prove a case against Marek."

Creasey looked as if he'd been slapped. "I knew it. I knew it yesterday, when the call came in at the station. It didn't feel right. The way everything else has gone against us . . . John, there's no doubt in your mind that he did it, is there?"

"That Marek killed Jennifer?"

"Yes."

He was entitled at least to that. "No, Sam. No doubt."

He hung his head, then shook it off and looked back at me. "I don't see Mrs. Daniels."

"I called her, but she said, all things considered, she wasn't up to seeing"—I gestured with my hand—"this."

"I think I know how she feels." He looked over to his wife, sitting ramrod straight in her bench. "I wonder if you'd mind sitting with us, with Tyne and me. I think Tyne would really appreciate it.

"Be glad to," I said.

We walked up to the front row, Creasey motioning for me to go in first. He whispered to me, "Could you sit on the other side of her, John? In case she faints or anything?"

I nodded and Creasey said gently. "Tyne, you remember John Cuddy. He came to the house about Jennifer."

Tyne looked up at me, then stared ahead

"Tyne," said Creasey in the same soft voice. "Let John past you, please?"

His wife shifted sideways, and I slid past and sat next to her. I and everyone else immediately had to stand as the court officer intoned, "Co-o-o-ourt. All rise."

The judge ascended the bench and the case was called by the clerk. As the audience settled back down, two uniformed sheriff's officers brought Marek in from a side door, no handcuffs. Marek was in a suit and looked marvelous despite his several jail meals. He smiled and shook hands with his attorney. As Gibson the prosecutor began speaking, Marek swung his head around, looked at me, and sneered, not ten feet away from us.

What came next takes a lot longer to relate than it did to happen. As Gibson paused for a question from the judge, I heard Creasey click open the videocassette case. I leaned forward to look at him across his wife, and he said quietly, "Tend to Tyne." Then Sam drew a short-barreled revolver from the case, stood up, and barked "Marek!" so sharply that the psychiatrist jumped while turning around to face us. Creasey pumped five shots into Marek as Marek's lawyer dived to the left and I threw my arms around Tyne and tackled her to the floor. Uniformed officers began firing at Sam, with several rounds either missing him or plowing through fleshy parts and lodging in the wall and bench around us. The impact of the slugs that definitely hit Creasey lifted him up and over the back of the pewlike seating, into the laps of the people behind us. There was a moment of stunned silence, smoke literally hanging in the air of the room. Then screams and yelling and everybody pushing and shoving as I helped Tyne back to a sitting position. She turned to me with that same vacant stare and said simply, "Thank you."

As I stood up, Bjorkman was craning over the aisle side of where Sam Creasey had fallen. I couldn't see the body, but Bjorkman, pointing with his gun barrel, said, "Those two there, the ones right above the heart. Those are mine."

I said, "Bjorkman?"

He turned that distorted baby face of his toward me, and I smashed his nose flat with my right fist. I had cocked my left when I heard Clay's voice say "Stupid shit," and then the lights went out.

"I should have seen it coming, kid."

How?

"The kind of man that Sam Creasey was, the way he talked with me about Texas justice, the camera guy letting on that Creasey had checked the videotapes personally that morning . . ."

Lean down.

I bent over, still a little rocky from Clay's competent sapping a few hours earlier. The afternoon breeze was cool, but when the wind stopped, the air had that faint oven glow that made summer seem imaginable, even close.

It's not your job to keep guns out of courtrooms. Or to keep people who have them from using them.

"Funny, I told Marek something like that. That it wasn't my job to see him hang, just so long as I got my client off."

How is William taking all this?

"Not too well when I saw him. He's pretty upset over the ride the system's given him."

It's not hard to see why he's bitter. Do you think he'll come through all this?

"I don't know. Maybe if Murphy took some more personalized interest in him."

Like a role model?

"Yeah."

Don't you think that maybe William has had enough of authority-figure role models? His brother, Marek . . .

"Me."

She tried to laugh. *It's hard to think of you as either an authority figure or a role model.*

"I guess I think of me as something else too."

And what's that?

"A Sam Creasey. Just a little luckier."

Creasey must have thought he didn't have anything left to live for. You do.

"Yeah."

I was just outside the cemetery gates and onto the sidewalk when I became peripherally aware of a red car slowly drawing even with me. I reflexively slid my right hand inside my jacket and back to my empty right hip. I hadn't remembered my gun when I'd picked up the car after court. I could feel more than see the driver leaning over and rolling down the passenger-side window. A wonderful voice said, "When I heard what happened at Middlesex this morning, I thought you'd come here."

I let out a breath and walked over to the Honda. Nancy Meagher smiled at me. Her hair was shorter, but everything else seemed the same. Which meant great.

"Good to see you again," I said.

"You too. How about a lift home?"

"My car's just a block away, and besides, I live way over in Back Bay."

Nancy smiled wider. "No, dunce. I meant a lift to *my* home."

I opened the door and climbed in.

Award-Winning Mystery Writer

Jeremiah Healy

Featuring DETECTIVE JOHN CUDDY

"One of the Best-Written Series
in the Field Today."
—*Bloomsbury Review*

☐ **SO LIKE SLEEP** ....64912/$3.50

☐ **THE STAKED GOAT** ....74284/$4.50

☐ **SWAN DIVE** ....67185/$3.95

☐ **YESTERDAY'S NEWS** ....69584/$4.50

**Available in Paperback
from Pocket Books.**

POCKET
B O O K S

Simon & Schuster Mail Order Dept.
200 Old Tappan Rd., Old Tappan, N.J. 07675

Please send me the books I have checked above. I am enclosing $_____ (please add 75¢ to cover postage
and handling for each order. Please add appropriate local sales tax). Send check or money order—no cash or
C.O.D.'s please. Allow up to six weeks for delivery. For purchases over $10.00 you may use VISA:
card number, expiration date and customer signature must be included.

Name _____

Address _____

City _____ State/Zip _____

VISA Card No. _____ Exp. Date _____

Signature _____
409

Pocket Books
Is Proud to Announce
the Publication of
Right to Die
A John Francis Cuddy Novel
by
Jeremiah Healy

Coming in Hardcover
from Pocket Books
July 1991

Please turn the page for an
exciting preview of *Right to Die*.

PART OF IT STARTED AS A DARE, SORT OF.

I was thinking how Massachusetts is crazy about giving its citizens days off for events it's not really observing. For example, the third Monday in April is known as Patriots' Day. Supposedly, the Commonwealth closes down to honor those who served in war. Actually, it just excuses us from work for the Boston Marathon. I once warned a friend who'd called me from Texas, a diehard Dallas Cowboys fan, that he'd have a tough time arriving here on Patriots' Day. Awed, he said, "Y'all have a holiday for your football team?" In fact, Suffolk County alone sets aside March 17 for the Wearing of the Green. The Irish pols neutrally dubbed that one "Evacuation Day," commemorating the momentous afternoon the colonists kicked the British troops out of Boston harbor. I've never mentioned Evacuation Day to the Texan; I'm afraid of what he'd think we were celebrating.

Nancy Meagher said, "God, it's freezing!"

She was standing in front of me, my arms joined around her. Or, more accurately, around the teal L. L. Bean parka over bulky ski sweater over long johns that she was wearing. On a brutal Saturday evening in early December we were waiting with forty thousand other hardy souls on Boylston Street, across from the elevated patio of the Prudential Center, for the lighting of the Christmas tree. A fifty-foot spruce is given to the city of Boston each year by the province of Nova Scotia. The gift commemorates something else, but without a masking holiday, I can never remember what it is.

A man on an accordion platform was adjusting a camera and klieg lights. Several hundred smarter folks watched from inside the windows of the Pru Tower or the new Hynes Convention Center. The smell of sausage and peppers wafted from somewhere near the Paris Cinema.

Nancy said, "Unconscionable."

"Sorry?"

"It is unconscionable not to start on time when it's this cold."

Hugging Nancy a little tighter, I looked around at our immediate neighbors. High school and college kids, not dressed sufficiently for the temperature, stamping their feet and stringing together ridiculous curses in the camaraderie of youth. Parents more my age, rubbing the mittened hands of their kids or wiping tiny red noses with wads of tissues pulled from pocket or handbag. A couple of cops in earmuffs, standing stoic but watchful. The crowd was well behaved so far, but occasionally you could hear coordinated shouting. If the Japanese restaurant behind and below us could have put up sake to go, they'd have made a fortune.

The weather really afflicted Nancy, but I was wearing just a rugby shirt under my coat and over my corduroy pants. Some Vikings must have come over the wall in my ancestors' part of County Kerry, because I rarely feel the winter.

To take Nancy's mind off it, I said, "You know, this is where the finish line used to be."

"The finish line?"

"Of the marathon."

No response.

I said, "The *Boston* Marathon?"

She cricked her neck to frown at me. Black hair, worn a little longer since autumn, wide blue eyes, a sprinkling of freckles across the nose and onto both cheeks. "Not all of us are day-labor private investigators, John Cuddy."

"Meaning?"

"Meaning I've lived in this city all my life, and I've never once seen the marathon in person."

"You're kidding?"

"It's too cold to kid."

"But the marathon's a holiday."

Nancy shrugged off my arms. "When I was little, traffic was too snarled to come over here from South Boston. When I was in law school, I thanked God for the extra day and studied."

"Nance, even the courthouse closes for the marathon. What's your excuse now?"

"I never knew anybody stupid enough to run that far."

"It's not stupid."

"It is."

"Is not."

She almost smiled. " 'Tis."

" 'Tain't."

"I suppose you think you could run it."

"I suppose I could."

"John, you're too big."

"Six two and a little isn't too big."

"I meant you're too heavy. The guys they show on TV are string beans."

"One ninety and a little isn't that heavy. Besides, I'd train down for it."

"John, anyway you're too . . ."

Nancy tried to swallow that last word, but I'd already heard it.

I said, "Too what?"

"Never mind."

"Too old, is what you said. You think I'm too old to run the marathon."

There was a feedback noise from an amplifier. Some "older" men were fiddling with a tall microphone on the patio under the tree. Then a male voice came over the public address system. "On behalf of the Prudential Center, I would like to welcome you to—"

The rest of his comments were drowned out by the swelling cheer of the crowd.

Over the roar I said into Nancy's ear, "Now it's down the street a couple of blocks."

"What?"

"I said, now it's down—"

"What is?"

"The finish line of the marathon. It used to be just about where we're standing. But when Prudential decided to scale back its operations here, the John

Hancock agreed to sponsor the race and moved the finish line down almost to the Tower." I pointed to the Hancock, a Boston landmark of aquamarine glass now known more for its sky deck than for the four-by-ten windows that kept sproinging out and hurtling earthward just after it was built.

Nancy didn't turn her head. "Fascinating. And still stupid."

At the mike a priest delivered a longish invocation. I let my eyes drift over to the Empire Insurance building. My former employer. I don't think Empire ever sponsored so much as a Little League team.

The priest was followed by our Mayor Flynn, who was blessedly brief in his remarks. Then the premier of Nova Scotia began an interminable speech that I couldn't follow. Nancy huddled back against me.

About ten feet from us, four guys wearing Boston College varsity jackets started a chant. "Light the fuckin' tree, light the fuckin' tree."

I laughed. Nancy muttered, "You're contemptible."

Finally, Harry Ellis Dickson, the conductor emeritus of the Boston Pops Orchestra, had his turn. He introduced Santa to much squealing and wriggling among the kids, many of whom were hoisted by dads and moms onto shoulders. Then Harry led the crowd through several carols. "O Come, All Ye Faithful," "Joy to the World," "Hark, the Herald Angels Sing." Everybody knew the first few lines, most of us dah-dah-ing the rest.

Between carols Nancy sighed. "We've become a one-stanza society."

Two slim figures in oddly modified Santa outfits danced up the steps of the patio.

Nancy said, "Who are they supposed to be?"

"Santa's eunuchs."

Again she shrugged off my arms. "I take it back. You're beneath contempt."

After a few more carols the star on top of the tree was lit, setting off a reaction in the crowd like the first firecracker on the Fourth of July. The long vertical strips of lights came on next. Then, beginning at the top, sequential clumps mixing red, blue, green, and yellow flashed to life, more a shimmer than individual bulbs, until the magic had hopped down the entire tree.

We finished with a universal "Silent Night," the crowd breaking up while the last notes echoed off the buildings.

"John! Gee, how long's it been?"

Tommy Kramer forgot to take the napkin off his lap as he rose to greet me. It fell straight and true to the floor. Only heavy cloth for Sunday brunch at Joe's American Bar & Grill.

"Tommy, good to see you."

He sat back, crushing a filterless cigarette in an ashtray but not noticing the napkin between his penny loafers. Moving upward, the flannel slacks were gray, the oxford shirt pale blue, the tie a Silk Regent with red background, and the blazer navy blue. Dressing down, for Tommy.

I took in the room's detailed ceilings and mahogany wainscoting, pausing for a moment on the bay window overlooking Newbury Street. The shoppers below bustled around half an hour before the boutiques would open for Christmas-season high rollers. We had a corner all to ourselves, the yuppies holding off until after twelve, when the booze could start to flow.

Tommy's rounded face seemed to lift a little, making him look younger. "You know, my old law firm used to own this place."

"I didn't know. The Boston one, you mean?"

"Right, right. Firm got started before the turn of the century, one of the first in the city to decide to make a Jew a partner. When word leaked out about that, the downtown eating clubs very politely told the firm's established partners, 'Well, you understand, of course, that we can't serve him here.' At which point the partners basically looked at each other, said 'fuck you' to the clubs, and bought a restaurant downtown for lunch meetings and this one here in Back Bay for dinner."

"So they could eat where they wanted."

"With whoever they wanted, including the new Jewish partner."

"The firm still run the place?"

"No, no. Sometime after I went out on my own in Dedham, they sold it. Back then, though, it was heady stuff for a young lawyer like me to be able to walk into one of the finest restaurants in Boston and be treated like the king of Siam."

"Your practice going well?"

"The practice? Oh, yeah, yeah. Couldn't be better. We're at eight attorneys now with the associate we brought in last week. Evening grad from New England."

Nancy's alma mater. "Kathy and the kids?"

"Terrific. She's gone and got her real estate ticket. Salesman, not broker yet, but that'll come in time. She's showing real estate all over town and having a ball. Slow market, like everywhere, but she knows the neighborhoods and the schools. Jason's on the wrestling team, Kit's doing indoor—oh, I get it. If everything's okay on the practice and home fronts, how come I drag you in here on ten hours notice?"

"Something like that."

A waitress in a tux came to the table and asked if we'd like to order. Both of us went with orange juice, eggs Benedict, and a basket of muffins.

When she was beyond earshot, Tommy said, "It's not for me. It's for somebody I owe."

Tommy's oblique way of reminding me that I still owed him for a favor.

"I'm listening."

He coaxed another cigarette from the Camel soft pack. "Okay if I . . . ?"

"The smoke doesn't bother me if the surgeon general doesn't bother you."

A match from the little box on the table flared, giving Tommy for an instant the look of a combat soldier, the curly hair still full enough to mimic a helmet. "Who would've thought, twenty, thirty years ago that someday you'd have to ask permission to light up?"

When I didn't say anything, he took a deep draw, then put the cigarette down, using the thumb and forefinger of his other hand to tweezer bits of tobacco from his tongue. "The guy approached me because he's not a lawyer himself, but he wants confidentiality in sounding you out."

"Tommy, the licensing statute requires me to

maintain the confidentiality of whatever the client tells me."

"Right, right. And this guy knows that. It's just . . . well, he wouldn't exactly be the client."

"Somebody wants to talk with me—"

"Wants me to talk with you—"

"But this somebody wouldn't be my actual client?"

"Right."

Our orange juice arrived. I sipped it. Fresh-squeezed, not from concentrate. Like the difference between chardonnay and Ripple. "Okay, I'm still listening."

"A friend of this guy is getting threats."

"Threats. Like over the telephone?"

"Like through the mail. Cut-and-paste jobs using words from magazines."

"The friend of the guy been to the police?"

"Not exactly."

"What exactly?"

"The secretary of the friend of the guy tried—"

"Tommy, this is getting a little out of hand. How about some real names."

He turned that over, shook his head. "How about some titles to make it easier?"

"Titles."

"Until you know whether you're interested or not."

"Okay. Titles."

Tommy pulled on the Camel, wisps of smoke wending out of his nostrils. "The guy I owe, let's call him the Activist. His friend who's getting the threats, let's call the friend the Professor. The Professor's secretary—"

"Tried going to the police."

"Right."

"And?"

"And the cops can't do much. I'm not into criminal law, but I'm assuming they checked the notes for fingerprints or postmarks and all, and came up empty."

"So you want me to do what?"

"I want you to talk to the Activist and the Secretary as my agent, if you're willing."

"As your agent."

"Right."

"Talk to them about what, bodyguarding the Professor?"

"No, no. She—they can talk to you more about that."

"Tommy . . ."

"Look, John, I know this sucks a little, but like I said, I owe the guy."

"The Activist."

"Right."

"Can you at least tell me how you owe this guy?"

Tommy took another puff. "When I was with that firm in Boston, they were real civil rights conscious."

"Good thing to be."

"Yeah, well, most of us young associates signed up as volunteers, whatever, for different causes through the BBA."

"Boston Bar Association?"

"Right, right. I drew . . ."

He stopped, took a puff out of sequence. "I drew this activist, and after I helped him out a couple of times, he started throwing a lot of business my way, business I really needed once I broke off on my own."

"Activist, Professor, Secretary."

"Huh?"

"Tommy, these don't sound like people who need the layers of confidentiality you're throwing up around them."

"John, that's kind of their business, don't you think?"

"Tommy, you want me to meet with them, it's kind of my business, don't you think?"

He put a casual look on his face, checking the room. "This activist, John, he's . . . Alec Bacall."

"Rings a bell somewhere."

"He's a gay activist, John."

Bacall. Majored in housing and employment rights, minored in AIDS issues. "Tommy, the professor here. Maisy Andrus?"

He flinched. "Keep your voice down, okay?"

"The right-to-die fanatic."

Tommy reddened. "She's not—" He caught himself speaking too loudly, our waitress thinking he meant her to come over. Tommy shook her off with an apologetic smile.

More quietly, Tommy said to me, "She's not a fanatic, John. She was a professor of mine, back in law school."

"At Boston College?"

"Right, right. Before she went over to Mass Bay."

I waited for Tommy to say something about my year as a student at the Law School of Massachusetts Bay. He didn't.

I said, "So Andrus was a professor of yours."

"And she helped me get that first job, at the law firm. Letter of recommendation, couple of phone calls, I found out later."

"So you owe her too."

"Yeah."

"And now she's being threatened."

Tommy ground out the cigarette. "Right."

"And she turns to you to turn to me."

"No, no, Alec—Bacall—is the one who called me."

I sat back. Watching him.

"What's the matter, John?"

"Quite a coincidence."

"Huh?"

"You contacting me to maybe help these people who preach the quick-and-happy ending."

Tommy looked very uncomfortable. Which was as good an answer as my next question could bring.

"John, look—"

"Tommy. I lost Beth to cancer, slowly. Bacall pushes the right to die for AIDS victims, Andrus casts a wider net. I'm the first one you think of?"

"John, I'm sorry. I should have . . . Look, I owe these people. From a long time ago, but I owe them. I once mentioned to Alec about Beth. Not directly, just that I could understand his position because I had a good friend who became a private investigator partly because his wife died. I never used your name or Beth's, it was just . . ."

"An example."

"Yeah. I'm sorry, but yeah. Then Alec calls me yesterday, and the guy's got a mind like a steel trap. He remembers me mentioning your situation, John. And he asks me to ask you."

Picking up my orange juice, I pictured Tommy dropping everything to help me with Empire and with Beth. To Tommy bailing me out when I was filling a hospital bed, a bullet hole in my shoulder and a skeptical D.A. on my neck.

"I'll talk to them."

"Great, great. Uh, John?"

"Yes."

"Today maybe?"

Nancy was at work, catching up on some research. After one more stop in the neighborhood, I'd be free for the afternoon.

"Two o'clock, Tommy. My office on Tremont Street."

"Alec said he'd be at the professor's house, so I'll call them now. I really appreciate this, John."

Getting up, Tommy got his feet tangled in the napkin and nearly fell into our waitress and eggs Benedict.